UNICORN OF GLASS

ELVA BIRCH

FAE SHIFTER KNIGHTS

Jingle bells and magic spells!

Fae Shifter Knights is a sizzling portal fantasy paranormal romance series with side-splitting humor, thrilling adventure, and heart. Each stand-alone novel features noble shifter heroes, brave and resourceful heroines who are fated to be their keys to magic in our world, adorable pets, and one bad-tempered, non-binary fae.

This book does stand alone, with a full character arc and a satisfying happy ever after, but it is part of a complete four-book series that will be most enjoyed in order:

Dragon of Glass (book 1)
Unicorn of Glass (book 2)
Gryphon of Glass (book 3)
Firebird of Glass (book 4)

CHAPTER 1

The Christmas bell by the door jingled as Heather came in, Vesta prancing happily at her feet. The holiday chime might be an odd sound to hear in July, but not nearly as odd as the Christmas music inside. Heather was sweating in the humid Georgia heat, even though they had only ducked out into it for a moment. Matters were not at all helped by the heavy green velvet 'elf' dress she was wearing. She peeled the fake fur back from her neck as she stepped into the frigid air conditioning.

It was probably ninety outside and comparatively it felt like fifty inside, though the thermostat behind the counter showed a perfectly livable seventy.

"I'm back!" Heather hollered towards the back of the store, pouring water from her bottle into the dog bowl underneath the register. Vesta lapped it up eagerly and crawled onto the pillow next to it, her wiry little tail beating out a rhythm as she settled down to nap at Heather's feet.

"We got a box!" Julie crowed, coming from the back

room of the shop just as Heather observed the delivery waiting on the counter. "Who gets to open it?"

Fred and Angie, the owners of the Ornament Shoppe, spent most of the summer touring the country in an RV, finding kitschy Christmas-themed treasure from all over the world in antique shops and at flea markets. Most of it came home with them in the fall in a trailer, but through the summer, they would ship some of it back.

Some of the things that Fred and Angie found defied belief: a horrifying wind-up laughing Santa Claus whose head popped off in a spray of red ribbons, a team of reindeer made entirely made of spoons and forks, a nativity scene made of metal dinosaurs, a can of Christmas turkey from the forties...and there were always new ornaments.

The Ornament Shoppe claimed it carried more ornaments than any other shop in the world, though Heather privately wondered if that was a statement that ever could or would be proven. It certainly had a *lot*. There were wooden ornaments, blown glass ornaments, metal ornaments, cheap plastic ornaments, popsicle-stick ornaments, cloth ornaments, papercraft ornaments, and balls of plastic and glass.

There was an entire aisle of Hallmark collectibles, and rows of weird geeky ornaments for television shows that had been off the air for decades, ethnic ornaments from all over the world, handmade ornaments, one-of-a-kind ornaments, even mechanical ornaments.

If there was an animal, no matter how obscure or imaginary, they had an ornament for it. If there was a hobby or sport, they had an ornament for it. They even had a Santaur ornament, with a half-horse, half-naked, disturbingly sexy Santa.

"It's your turn for the honor," Heather said with a sigh.

"I'll watch the register. But if you find any Italian Greyhounds, I need to know."

"You know I'm always looking out for the Iggies," Julie said. She leaned over the counter. "Hi, Vesta."

Vesta gave a whine in greeting, her little tail wagging faster, and she scrambled to her feet.

"No jumping," Heather cautioned her, as the tiny dog appeared to be gauging the distance up to the counter. Italian Greyhounds frequently thought they could fly, and Heather wasn't sure her heart or her wallet could take a broken leg.

Vesta eyed Heather, testing her resolve, and when Heather stared her down, gave a large sigh for her small frame and lay down on the floor to sulk.

Julie hefted the box as the door bells announced a new cluster of customers. "Have fun," she said, winking as she walked away, the skirt of her own elf costume bouncing as she went.

"Hi," Heather called to the party that had just entered. It was a group of middle-aged women who looked overheated and uninterested. Heather wasn't sure if they were looking for something in particular—the shop didn't do much business in July—or if they were just looking for a place more interesting than a grocery store that had air conditioning to pace around in and gossip. "Welcome to the Ornament Shoppe. Let me know if you need any help finding anything!"

They gave her the expected polite murmurs of dismissal and vanished back into the aisles. Heather could hear them complaining about the weather and the traffic and their children.

She was sorting receipts and wondering if the air conditioner in her apartment would be working when she got home when they re-emerged, their conversation having shifted to catty gossip about someone who wasn't with them. One of them had a clearance box of Christmas cards to purchase. Another had found an ornament they wanted and was carrying it carefully in their hands.

"Francine is crazy about unicorns," the woman said, laying it down on the counter after their friend had finished their purchase. "She's going to love this."

Heather completely forgot about the receipts she was sorting, her apartment, the itchy velvet she was wearing, and the small dog lying near her feet.

It was an ornament she hadn't seen before, a blue, blown glass unicorn rearing in a ring of white glass, and she knew beyond a shadow of a doubt that it had to be *hers*.

"I can't sell you that," she blurted.

The customers stared at her.

"I'm sorry," she stammered, scrambling for a reason more coherent than simply *that's mine and you can't have it.* "That…ah…wasn't supposed to go out on display. It's being…it's reserved! I'm so sorry for the mixup! We have a few more unicorns in stock, I think. I can look them up in the computer for you."

The customer, a thin woman with an expensive haircut, looked confused and disgusted. "I wanted this one," she said defensively, and she made a quick motion like she was going to pick the ornament back up.

Heather's blood roared in her ears and her heart pounded as she stepped forward to snatch it away. "You can't have it!"

Unfortunately, she managed to step directly onto Vesta's tail, and the Italian Greyhound gave a yelp of surprise and pain and scurried out from under the counter as Heather, trying to catch herself before her full weight was down on the dog's tail, made a dive for the ornament.

The customer had picked up the gold thread it was hanging on, but Heather had her fingers on the glass, and for a split second, her entire world went away. All she could hear was a ringing battle call, and she was surrounded by pure light and…a compelling presence. Out of the light, there was a draft horse-sized unicorn, white neck arching as he lowered his gleaming golden horn towards her.

Her entire body was on fire, and she was filled with longing.

Julie's voice broke the spell. "What the hell, Heather?"

Heather managed to pry her fingers from the cool glass and the ornament she'd yanked away from the customer fell a scant inch to the counter top. "I don't know," she gasped. The ornament appeared to have survived the drop without damage, but Heather didn't dare pick it up or touch it again.

Vesta was whining at her feet, and the gaggle of customers on the other side of the counter was looking at her like she'd lost her mind.

Which, Heather had to admit, was a distinct possibility.

"I wanted *this* ornament," the client whined.

Julie looked from her to Heather. "It's not for sale," she said firmly. "I'm happy to find you another similar one."

"I don't want another one," the thin woman complained. "I want *this one*. I want to talk to the manager about this."

"I'm the manager," Julie bluffed. "This ornament wasn't supposed to be put out. I'm very sorry to disappoint you. Can I offer you a Christmas in July postcard?"

Barely mollified, the customers took their purchases and glossy cards and stomped back out to their cars.

Heather was keenly aware of Julie's concerned gaze but her own eyes kept being drawn back to the ornament on the counter.

"Thanks," Heather said, when she'd finally caught her breath. "I'm not really sure what happened."

Julie reached over her, and before Heather could warn her away, had picked up the ornament. "It's pretty, but I'm not sure what the big deal about it is. I didn't know you were unicorn-crazy."

And nothing happened to her.

Heather waited for the swooning and the flushing, but Julie only frowned at the sparkling glass piece.

"I...I don't know, maybe I had a hallucination or something," Heather said weakly. "I just knew that the ornament was mine, and then I...saw..." She couldn't quite admit that she'd had a bizarre vision of a *unicorn*.

"You've been pulling long days," Julie observed with concern. "Did you get heatstroke walking Vesta? Maybe you should head home early."

Heather reached down to where Vesta was trying to get her attention and picked up the wriggling dog. "Sorry about your tail, sweetie," she told the greyhound, who proved her forgiveness with her tongue. "I've been drinking only water, I promise," she told Julie. "But maybe the nonstop Christmas music finally gave me a psychotic break. I think I *will* go home early."

"Don't forget your unicorn," Julie said, and Heather could only stare at it. *Her unicorn.*

"Do you want me to wrap it up for you?" Julie offered after an awkward pause.

"Yeah," Heather said in relief. "Could you?"

Julie wrapped the ornament carefully in tissue paper and tucked it into a box while Heather gathered up Vesta's leash and toys, trying not to be too obvious about her anxiousness while Julie casually handled the fragile ornament and put it into a bag. Heather paid the price on the tag out of her purse.

"Stay cool," Julie called, as she finally left, opening the door out into the sweltering heat.

Heather thought wryly that it was far too late for that.

* * *

Rez felt the touch, the seductive caress of fingers over his glass prison, and his first instinct was to fall into a stupor of happiness.

The knight's second impulse was to strike out, because there was clearly magic at work here, and magic had betrayed his shieldmates.

He didn't trust either inclination, but he knew, in a dazed way, that everything was *wrong*. He was nowhere and everywhere, floating in a haze of light that lit nothing. There were no limbs to command to kick, human or unicorn, and he was distressingly *powerless*.

It was easiest to concentrate on *her*.

She was not powerless, as was obvious by her effect on Rez. The spell felt subtle, convincing in its gentle persuasion. All he had to do was relax, embrace the promise of her presence, and she would free him…

Which was entirely too good to be true, and Rez had seen too much deceit to believe such absurd tales. It was a *trap*.

He would resist her with the last strength left within him.

CHAPTER 2

*H*eather kicked the door shut behind her and groaned as she put her bag and purse on the table and Vesta on the cheap vinyl tile. The greyhound went prancing across the room with a cheerful clack of her toenails to greedily drink from her water dish.

"Sure, you've got energy," Heather griped. "You didn't have to walk up three flights of stairs wearing *velvet* when it's ninety degrees."

Her apartment was as hot inside as it was outside, and it smelled stuffy on top of that. Heather muttered curse words under her breath as she went to inspect the air conditioner. Pressing buttons did nothing. She growled and went to the kitchen, where the fuse box was hidden behind a wall quilt of polar bears and penguins.

She envied anyone who got to live on a block of ice right now.

Sure enough, the fuse in question had been blown. Heather flipped the switch, and the air conditioner grumbled to life...for about ten seconds.

Snap!

The fuse tripped off again while she was watching it.

Heather swore under her breath, then switched the fuse again. "Come on, come on, come on," she begged as the air conditioner wheezed and tried to start.

Snap!

"Motherfu-" Heather bit back her expletive and stomped to her purse to dig out her phone.

"Whaaaaah?" her landlord answered impatiently. Was he drunk?

"Hi, Marcus," Heather said as brightly as she could manage. "Heather, of apartment 35. The air conditioner is blowing the fuse. Again."

Marcus swore more creatively than Heather had. "Didja let it cool off?" His words were slurred, confirming her guess.

"Believe me," Heather said as calmly as she could manage. "It hasn't been running all afternoon. It's ninety degrees in here." She didn't think she was exaggerating, but since the thermostat readout didn't work either, she couldn't check.

"When I can," Marcus grudgingly promised.

"I appreciate it," Heather said through gritted teeth. "Sooner would be better."

Marcus muttered something non-committal and hung up.

"Same to you, jerk face," Heather said to the dead line.

She tugged at the neck of her dress, desperate for the merest hint of a draft between her sweaty skin and the cloying velvet.

Vesta, not the slightest bit bothered by the heat, jumped up onto the table and nosed at the bag from The Ornament Shoppe.

Her unicorn, Heather remembered abruptly. Her magical unicorn ornament.

She unwrapped in carefully, wondering if the tingle of anticipation was anything more than her own unexplainable excitement. She remembered the vision she'd had, and more than that, the desire that had threatened to swamp her.

Was it just a crazed manifestation of the fact that she'd been living like a nun for far too long? Had she been drugged? She hadn't taken anything stronger than an ibuprofen in weeks, but maybe she'd walked through some kind of...experimental chemical discharge on her way to the parking lot. Maybe it was *magic*.

Every option that she could think of was nuttier than the last.

So, maybe she'd only imagined the whole thing.

Except that...

The beautiful ornament lay in a nest of tissue paper in her hands, and Heather felt like she was being pulled to it, irresistibly. She wanted to touch it, she yearned to see the unicorn again.

She felt like it was *begging* her to caress it.

Magic.

It was definitely *magic*.

It was July, and a magical Christmas ornament was begging for her touch.

"Well, Vesta," she finally said, "I'm either nuts or this is the start of a very confused Hallmark holiday movie."

Well, she knew how those played out. And it usually started with a *kiss*.

Without letting her fingers touch it, she closed her eyes, raised it to her mouth and gave it a brief, feather-light brush of her lips.

The kiss began with the cool touch of glass that she expected, then light flashed against her closed eyelids. Vesta gave a yip of surprise and Heather opened her eyes to find herself nose-to-nipple with a broad expanse of sculpted chest.

CHAPTER 3

The touch of her perfect mouth broke the spell with a bell-like tone that Rez was sure must ring through the entire fallen kingdom.

He knew at once that he was somewhere completely alien; he was in a strange room with several windows of remarkably smooth glass panes. There was a padlocked door, and a short hallway leading to more open doors. Odd benches and boxes cluttered the room. The furniture was all finely crafted, and the couch was covered in a tapestry of gold and green.

It was uncomfortably hot and humid and a small gray hound was cavorting at his feet, its tiny nose twitching in curiosity.

None of his shieldmates were nearby, and Rez felt that loss like the cut of a knife. Did the woman before him have something to do with their disappearance, or was her seduction of him independent of their downfall?

Because there was no doubt that she was attempting to seduce him.

She was standing an unseemly distance from him, so

close that he could feel her breath against his chest, and he looked directly down onto the swells of her breasts above a low-cut dress in the richest of green velvets trimmed with white fur. Her rich, sepia skin looked as touchably soft as her dress, and her wide brown eyes were pools of warmth and wonder.

He was drawn to her in a way that was simply impossible.

Impossible without magic.

Rez reached down into his own magic half, calling on his unicorn to provide a counterspell...and found nothing.

No, not *nothing*, but the wellspring of power that he had expected was the merest of trickles and it dissolved as soon as he touched it. She had *stolen* his power.

Panic gripped him.

He was in a strange place, with no magic, being twined into a spell so subtle and strong that it felt like it was coming from his own loins.

He may not have power, but he was not completely helpless; his human body seemed to have suffered no harm during his entrapment. Even with no sword…

Rez reached out and captured the woman by her arms.

"Release me," he growled, leaning close to convince her of his threat.

It backfired terribly.

Her arms were strong and soft, and the touch of her did dire things to long-neglected parts. Her beautiful face, this close, begged him to finish the kiss that she'd started, and Rez found his traitor thumbs trying to caress her arms rather than shake her into submission.

He would have a sword of sorts in no time at all if he did not get her away from him, but before he could force himself to let go, there was a pounding on the door and the tiny hound at their feet began to bay.

"I have never been *less* grateful for prompt attention from Marcus," the woman breathed. She sidled back and Rez could make himself unhand her.

"You can't be here like this," the woman said, shaking her head. Was she breathing hard because of the effort the spell was costing her?

She looked around in alarm, then put the tissue-wrapped bundle she was holding down and pulled a woven blanket from the back of a plush chair, thrusting it at Rez. "Wait in the bedroom," she said firmly, and Rez numbly let her crowd him back down the hallway towards an open door.

The pounding on the outer door occurred again, this time with a string of curse words. "Do you want your goddamn air conditioner fixed or not, *Heather of apartment 35*? I got better things to be doing."

Heather of Apartment 35 was apparently the title for this woman, and she opened the door to a soft-looking, pale-haired man with a vile scowl and the sour smell of alcohol. Rez immediately dismissed him as a threat and categorized him as *nuisance*.

"Marcus," she greeted him.

Heather of Apartment 35 had some purpose for him, and let him grudgingly in. Rez hung back in the shadow of the hallway, watching and waiting, the blanket still in his hands.

The visitor did not seem to notice him, or anything other than the alluring woman in her short-skirted dress, pointing out the *thing* he was clearly meant to service. A wizard of some kind? He had a silver box with a handle on the top that must contain the tools of his trade.

The small hound milled at their feet and sniffed things.

They spoke in code, of fuses and circuits and things being blown.

"Are you sure you should be doing this right now?" Heather of Apartment 35 was clearly expressing doubts of his ability to cast in his condition that Rez privately agreed with. Magic should always be done with a clean mind, not muddied by inebriating substances.

"You want your goddamn air conditioner fixed or not?" Marcus retorted. He fumbled with his box and had difficulty kneeling to inspect the item in question without staggering sideways. He seemed to be spending most of his energy ogling down the sorceress' dress when she bent carelessly, and Rez could feel a growl rise in his throat at his crude attention.

She was clearly uninterested and annoyed, and Rez wondered that Marcus did not fear her wrath. Perhaps he was too *impaired* to have judgment.

Marcus managed to move the silver box a little ways away, and then asked the sorceress to retrieve a specific tool.

When she innocently knelt to assist, Marcus started to move back so that he had a view up her skirt, and something in Rez snapped.

"Return your eyes to their place, or I will cover them for you permanently," he snarled, stepping out of the hallway, just as the woman startled away from the interloper and pulled down her skirt with a fiery glare.

"Whoa," Marcus said, staring.

Rez, unarmed and unclothed, had no doubt of his ability to overcome this puny man. He snapped the blanket he was still holding in the air and closed the distance between them with two strong strides.

Marcus tumbled backwards. "I'm sorry, man, I didn't know you were here…"

"What kind of man needs the presence of another to remind him of that which is appropriate?" Rez scoffed.

Marcus blinked without understanding.

"I will make it easier for you, since you are clearly incapable of controlling yourself," Rez growled. "Heather of Apartment 35 is now under my protection. If you so much as leer in her direction, I will break every bone in your body and leave you in a waterless desert to die."

Marcus was scooting backwards away from him, sobering swiftly in his terror. "I didn't do nothing," he insisted desperately. "Who'd want to?" he bluffed, then he crawled away faster.

The small gray hound barked and capered at the feet of her mistress.

Rez followed Marcus across the room to the door, where he pulled himself up on the doorframe and fled. Rez closed it firmly behind him.

CHAPTER 4

*A*s much as Heather loved watching Marcus flee her apartment in terror, as rewarding as it was to have a gorgeous hunk stick up for her honor, this was just *weird*.

Also, this complete stranger was still very real and large and incredibly *nude*, which made forming words unbelievably difficult.

And her air conditioner wasn't fixed.

"That was...something," she managed to squeak. "I, er, thanks." She bent down to scoop Vesta into her arms.

Huge-and-gorgeous managed to ratchet things up another notch by kneeling at her feet rather abruptly. "I beseech you, release me. Return me to my shieldmates."

"I'm...um...not sure how to do either of those things," Heather said, looking down at the top of his head. He had long, thick brown hair, highlighted in gold, and his shoulders were broad and knotted with muscles. He looked up at her with silvery-blue eyes under eyelashes that mascara models only wished they had. "Maybe we should start with names."

"Rez," he said, sounding defeated. "I am Rez, unicorn

knight, protector of the realm, defender of the fallen crown."

"Is it okay to just call you Rez, or do I need to use all of that?" Heather asked.

"Rez would honor me," he agreed. "You are Heather of Apartment 35."

"Just Heather is fine," she said breathlessly, because he seemed to think that an exchange of names allowed him to climb to his feet again.

He was simply magnificent, broad and chiseled, his face as ruggedly handsome as his amazing physique. His skin was tawny, his features without any origin that Heather could quite put her finger on.

"This is Vesta," she introduced, because the greyhound was squirming in her arms. "She's an Italian Greyhound."

"She looks like an admirable ratter," Rez said. He did not offer to pet her.

"We...ah...don't have a lot of rats," Heather said. "She's just a companion." She put the dog down.

Vesta scampered to sit adoringly at Rez's feet and gaze up at him until he knelt and stroked her sleek head and body obediently. No one could resist Vesta for long.

"Can you explain how I am here, and...where *is* here?" he asked plaintively, and if he had been appealing as a gorgeous, naked gladiator rushing to defend her honor, he utterly melted her panties with his small lost voice as he gently greeted her dog.

"I don't know," Heather admitted. "I mean, this is Fairburn, a suburb of Atlanta, Georgia, in the United States of America, on the planet Earth, and I suspect that basically none of that will mean anything to you."

He shrugged in mute agreement.

"That's what I figured," Heather said. "I'll tell you what I know."

She walked to the table where she'd left the unicorn ornament, still cradled in tissue, and held it up by the string.

"I work in a shop that sells ornaments," she said. "Someone tried to buy this, but I wouldn't—couldn't—sell it to them. I had to have it for myself, and when I touched it, I had this...vision. I saw..." It felt supremely stupid to say she'd seen a unicorn, even in a world where gorgeous naked men suddenly appeared by magic.

"You saw me," Rez said, his voice low and sexy.

"I saw a *unicorn*," Heather said. Yup, that sounded as ridiculous out loud as it had sounded in her head.

"You saw *me*," Rez repeated.

Heather stared at him and tried to decide how being utterly insane could make him somehow even *more* sexy.

"You're a unicorn?" she scoffed. "I mean, in the pointy-horned, four-legged, golden-hoofed sense?"

"I am a unicorn knight."

As if it were as normal as butter on toast.

"Moving on," Heather said. "I brought the ornament home, called my drunk jerk of a landlord because the air conditioner keeps tripping the fuse, and then..." Saying that she'd kissed a glass ornament sounded as foolish in her head as seeing a unicorn.

"You kissed me." Rez didn't say it like he exactly *appreciated* it. More like he was suspicious of it.

"Sure," Heather said swiftly. "And I guess it broke your spell or something, because *bam*, naked man in my living room. As if it wasn't already hot enough with the air conditioning broken." *I should have kept that to my inside voice.*

He eyed her untrustingly.

Heather sighed. "Okay, then, it's your turn. Where are you from, and why were you in that ornament?"

"I am a protector of the broken crown..." Rez rose. "But I would have to go back further than that to explain."

"I got all day, honey," Heather said. She immediately wished that she hadn't called him *honey*. "You want some tea?"

Rez nodded, but looked quite put out when she poured him a glass of iced tea from the fridge. "It is...cold?"

"Do you *want* hot tea in this weather?" Heather sat at the kitchen table and waved him into the other chair. To her gratitude, he wrapped the blanket he was holding around his waist for an illusion of modesty.

"No, lady," he said solemnly as he sat. "Have you...a portal to somewhere colder in that box?"

A *portal?*

"Ah, no. No portals here. No magic, generally, actually. We have machines and things that are supposed to make our lives easier but mostly break down and cost a lot to repair." He was a lot less distracting safely sitting, Heather thought.

"Marcus," Rez surmised, looking at the toolbox he'd left behind.

"Yeah, he owns my apartment," Heather said sourly. "He is *supposed* to be in charge of fixing my things, but that doesn't always happen."

"Ah," Rez said. He had drained the tea and was trying to get the sugar from the bottom using his fingers. "Marcus appears to be a *lesser* kind of man."

Heather nearly snorted her tea. "Yeah, you could say that."

"I thought at first that he might be ridden," Rez said dismissively, licking the sugar from his fingers in a way that made Heather uncomfortably aware again that he was naked underneath the blanket he was wearing like a kilt. "But he was merely foolish and inebriated."

"Ridden?" she squeaked, thinking entirely too hard about things she'd like to ride.

Rez's dark look and dire tone squashed those thoughts. "Does this world have dours?"

"What are dours?" Heather asked, already dreading his answer from his expression.

"They appear like shadows, but no light casts them. They can possess a man, turning his darkest thoughts into action. They make him greedy, angry, fearful. They turn neighbors against each other, make friends into enemies, incite jealousy. When a dour takes a man's mind, they bend it to evil, but it is without aim. They are wild, chaotic magic. More dangerous are bleaks, which can control these dours for their own nefarious purposes. You...do not have those, either?"

"Bleaks?" Heather shook her head slowly. "Not by that name."

"They are half-shadow, half-man, as I am half-magic, half-man. My shieldmates and I are light to their dark."

"Who are your shieldmates?" Heather had to ask.

"My fellow knights," Rez said mournfully. "Trey, Henrik, Tadra, and our teacher, Robin. We are...were...the last of our kind, the final protectors of a fallen world."

"A...fallen world?"

"We knew that the battle we faced was likely to be our last," he said grimly. "The bleaks on my world were led by a powerful man of shadow and magic, and...I had doubts of our long-term success." He reached forward and fingered the unicorn ornament on the table. "I wish I knew what has happened to them, but I fear the worst."

Broody Rez was more dangerous to Heather's peace of mind than even lost Rez, and she was once again keenly aware that he wasn't wearing a stitch beneath her afghan.

She put her iced tea down on the table hard enough that the ring around the ornament clinked against the unicorn.

They both stared at it in alarm for a moment, both undoubtedly wondering what would happen to Rez if the ornament broke.

"If you're going to be in this world for a little while, you're going to need clothing," she said firmly.

"It is warm enough that garments are not necessary," Rez said off-handedly.

Heather opened her mouth to protest that it was *very necessary indeed*, then realized that his silvery eyes were dancing. He knew *exactly* what his body was doing to her.

And playful Rez was the sexiest yet.

Heather badly needed to escape, before she did something she regretted, like rip off her sweaty elf costume and throw herself at him. "I'm going to go down the hall and see if I can borrow some clothes from a friend of mine who is nowhere near your size, but still way closer than I am."

Rez stood at the same time she did, and the blanket slid entirely too far down for comfort before he caught it.

"I'll be back," she squeaked. Or possibly, she said something closer to "Ibba baaaaah yeah…"

She fled out of the apartment and heard Vesta bark in dismay as the door shut behind her.

CHAPTER 5

*R*ez knew that his first goal must be to break the spell of Heather of Apartment 35.

Her magic allure diminished with her exit, and Rez was able to finally think almost clearly again. He still yearned for her, but he could remind himself that this was merely part of her enchantment.

He looked out the window over the broken box that had been the focus of attention. All he could see was the side of another building, with the same strange windows. He could hear distant growls of great beasts, and a dull chaos of beeps and bells and far-off voices. The sliver of sky that he could see was hazy with heat.

Vesta, distraught by her mistress' absence, whined and trembled and came to Rez's feet. She placed tiny paws on his leg and begged for comfort. Before Rez could stop himself, he had scooped the hound into his arms as he'd seen Heather do, and cuddled her close.

Obviously, the witch's spell had been cast to include her companion.

Vesta stopped quivering and butted her head into his

chest in delight. Her whip-like tail beat a cheerful rhythm on his arm.

Rez frowned down at her. He needed to find how the sorceress did her casting and undo her evil work.

Vesta looked at him with huge, adoring eyes and Rez knew that he needed to hurry, before he lost more of himself.

He put the hound down firmly and scowled down the hallway. Magic was usually kept to private chambers; it was unlikely that she cast spells in rooms where she entertained. He opened the first door to find a shallow closet filled with bedding and furs and boxes marked 'Christmas' and 'Games.' There were several shelves of unmarked containers. A quick rummage of their contents showed unusual items and a rather alarming amount of yarn, but none of it appeared magical.

There was a tall machine in the bottom with hoses and ropes, but Rez could not make sense of it, and when he tipped it over with a vicious jab, it merely lay on the floor.

The next door was far more fruitful.

Here was a tiled room with an uncomfortable-looking chair, a sink with a small hand-pump on it, and tall glass walls enclosing a shining space.

Rez had never seen anything like it, but it was clearly a space for ritual. There were furs of unnaturally colorful animals hanging on racks, and there was a mirror above the wash basin, undoubtedly for scrying. His reflection glowered back at him.

He drew fingers along the edge of the mirror, wishing with all his might for the power to see his shieldmates.

The mirror refused to obey him and the power he could barely sense fizzled away as fast as he tried to touch it.

Vesta, capering at his feet, found one of the colorful

furs on the floor and burrowed into it eagerly. Rez crouched and discovered that although it was *furry*, it did not actually appear to be fur. Vesta growled and chewed on the fabric, inviting him to play with her.

Rez reminded himself that he was there to break free of his fascination with the hound and her mistress.

There was a thick L-shaped tool on the counter by the mirror, tethered to the wall with smooth rope. Rez picked it up, turning it in his hands. It appeared to be hollow on one side, the interior covered with a grate. Was something trapped within it?

As he peered into it, his hand slid along a button on the other side of the device and there was a sudden roar and a blast of fiery air, directly into his eyes. Rez flung the thing away from him, and the rope attaching it to the wall came loose and whipped after it with a pronged tail.

The roar silenced in an instant, and after a moment, Rez cautiously picked it up again.

The creature inside had been subdued. Or perhaps it had escaped in that moment. The device was warm to the touch.

More careful now, Rez inspected the glass chamber. One of the panels slid to the side, and he carefully stepped inside. This was clearly a place of magic, the strong smells of flowers and spices almost overwhelming here. There were bottles of her spell ingredients standing on a shelf. There were knobs on the wall, and a metal serpent with a cylindrical face frozen in place above them.

Vesta did not offer to come into the sacred chamber with him, standing outside with her tail wagging.

Rez opened each bottle in turn, hoping for a clue in the scents, but each was filled with some kind of rich liquid, and he had no idea what combination would undo what she had cast. In the end he replaced the lids and left the chamber altogether, Vesta at his heels.

Would it be so bad to fail? he wondered as he went to the last door in the hallway.

He had been fighting for so long, so uselessly. The promise of peace in her warm eyes, in her warm skin, in her warm embrace...was it wrong of him to want that?

It was hard to think ill of Heather, his senses clouded by his need for her. It would be so easy, to give in and let her seduce him into her arms…and her bed.

This last room was clearly a sleeping chamber. A wide bed was covered in decadent pillows and silky-looking sheets and light blankets. For a moment, Rez could do nothing but imagine laying Heather down on that bed, her beautiful skin dark against the pale sheets, her hair spread on the pillow beneath her. It took all of his self-discipline to turn away and wrestle himself back into control.

There were bookshelves all along the walls, and Rez drew his fingers along the spines, reading the titles.

It was a wide range of titles and topics, and he drew one down at random: "Tales of the Fae."

CHAPTER 6

Heather had been so dazzled by her naked unicorn knight from another world that she had forgotten to take her key with her, so she stood outside her own apartment and knocked.

It took so long for Rez to answer the door that for a moment Heather had a moment of panic wondering if she actually had imagined the whole thing. She dreaded trying to track down Marcus to let her back in.

Then Rez was sweeping the door open and Vesta was prancing forward to greet her with whines and yips of joy.

Heather barely noticed her, staring at Rez.

She was pretty sure she wasn't imagining him simply because her imagination had never been so generous with her. He was like a god, or a gladiator.

"I borrowed you some clothes," she tried to say. It sounded more like, "Ahh baaaaaah waaaaaah…"

She settled for thrusting the pants and shirt she was holding at him, and bending to greet Vesta with a back scratch to cover her confusion. Bending over, unfortunately, put her at eye level with Rez's considerable...attributes. At some point, he'd lost the afghan kilt.

She straightened so swiftly that she nearly fell over, and Rez steadied her with a hand on her arm that felt like an electric shock.

"These are curious garments," Rez said, unfolding them.

"Beggars can't be choosers," Heather attempted. It was mostly stuttering and long vowels again. The sooner this man got dressed, the sooner she'd be able to manage words again.

He pulled on the sweatpants and t-shirt while she looked fixedly away. They mostly fit, to Heather's relief. The sweats were a little snug and short, and the t-shirt was tight in the shoulders and otherwise loose. Instead of looking less sexy, Rez just looked tantalizing.

"I have discovered your library," he said. "And I have perhaps uncovered some clues about where I am from."

Heather looked at the book that he'd found, knotting her brows in curiosity. "That's...fiction," she cautioned him. Then she remembered that he'd been caught in a glass ornament, and was, allegedly, half unicorn, and nothing seemed too crazy.

"Does your world also have stories that have seeds of truth?" Rez asked.

Heather thought wryly about the news, and about fairy tales. "You could say that."

"This book talks about a place of fae, beyond a veil, where a royal court of magic users rules. A world that lacks your strange technology. This...may describe my world. Though I swear on my honor that I have not and would not steal children."

Heather looked at him and had a pang of sympathy for him that trumped her feelings of lust. He was all alone in a strange, alien world, looking for a purpose, a reason to be here, of all places.

Then she looked past him. "What did you do to my vacuum cleaner?" she demanded.

The closet door was open, the vacuum on its side in the hallway.

"I do not believe it came to harm," Rez said. "But I may have released the creature from your workshop."

"Creature in my…okay, you know what, it is too hot to think. Marcus left his toolbox, I'm going to change my clothes and see if I can fix the air conditioner myself, and you can tell me more about this magical world that you came from."

Heather changed swiftly in the bathroom, picking her hair dryer up off the floor in confusion. She splashed herself with cool water and slipped into a pair of shorts and a tank top.

Rez's reaction to her was gratifying; his eyes on her were hot and full of desire. He set his teeth, like he was trying to be angry with her. "Is it seemly to dress thusly?" he inquired.

"This is far more normal than the green velvet," Heather assured him. "You probably shouldn't use me as a benchmark for modern fashion." She wondered what he'd think when she dressed up for her Ren Faire job in a few days, then realized it was unlikely that he would still be there in a few days. If there was really a fairy queen, she was going to want this beautiful slab of a knight back.

The Internet assured her that her air conditioner causing the fuse to blow was most likely caused by a short, and described several solutions that sounded like they were actually in her realm of expertise. Rez asked her the names of all the items in her apartment, and she absently answered him.

While she took the cover off of the unit, Rez told her about his shieldmates.

"Are you all unicorns?" Heather asked. A world of unicorn fairy hunks didn't sound all bad.

"No, my brothers are a dragon and a gryphon and my sister is a firebird. Our teacher is Robin, a fable."

"Sounds like a fun family reunion," Heather quipped.

"I miss them," Rez said solemnly. "We trained together our entire lives. In vain."

Heather didn't have an answer for that.

"What is it you are doing?" Rez asked, looking over her shoulder at the tangle of wires and circuit boards she had exposed.

"So, when this thing turns on, it trips the breaker, so it's drawing more energy than it ought to be, because...okay, do you know what electricity is?"

"I do not," Rez confessed.

He was kneeling very close to her, and even clothed, his presence made Heather think of a very different kind of electricity. "It's...ah...an energy source," she explained. "It comes from wires that are running in the walls that connect to a big central power plant."

"Like magic," Rez suggested.

"Well, it's not," Heather floundered. "It's made using science, and it's run to our houses and comes out from these outlets here."

Rez started to put his finger towards the holes.

"No!" Heather warned him. "It's dangerous. Too big an electric shock can kill you."

"Like magic," Rez repeated, but he pulled his hands back respectfully.

"So electricity has to follow a path, through these wires. If you disrupt the path, it just stops. And in this case, if you have a short—that's a place a wire crosses where it shouldn't—then you end up with surge of electricity that trips the breaker, and that *breaks* the path for the electricity."

"Why have a breaker?" Rez asked, and he was so close to Heather that her own brain was shorting out a little.

"Because if too much energy runs through wires, they get really hot, and they can...cause fires."

There were fires now, in the pit of Heather's stomach, and lower, and Rez was leaning even closer.

"I must find a way to *break* your spell," he said, and then he reached out and dragged a reluctant finger down the side of her face.

"My spell?" Heather whispered, the air conditioner entirely forgotten. "There's no magic here. No magic but you."

"There is," Rez insisted. "I can feel it, just out of reach. And I can feel the allure you've cast on me."

"I promise, I haven't cast anything on you," she insisted, the path of his finger wildly alive. "I wouldn't know how."

It would have taken the slightest lean forward to kiss him, barely even an effort, and Heather desperately wanted to. She wanted to slide her arms up around those beautiful shoulders, twine her fingers into his soft hair. She wanted his arms crushing her, and his mouth against hers.

And she thought that he might want her, too.

But there was *crazy*, and then there was kissing a hot stranger who came out of a magic glass ornament *crazy*.

She turned back to the air conditioner.

CHAPTER 7

When Rez expected her to demand the kiss he was ready to surrender to, she surprised him by drawing away.

"Oh look," she breathed. "There's the short."

Rez could make no sense of what he was seeing, but the *wires* and *circuit boards* that she pointed out must have made sense to Heather.

"I'm lucky this thing didn't burst into flames," she muttered.

Rez retreated enough that she could manage to untangle the mess and carefully peel away the damaged plastic from the wires. Marcus' toolbox had an assortment of specialized tools that she used to cut and strip the wires back to undamaged sheathing.

He watched her in confusion and awe. He had been ready to succumb to her wiles, and if he was any judge, she had wanted him as badly as he wanted her. But she had turned her face away, rather than accept his capitulation.

Was it possible that she had *not* enchanted him? Could some greater force be at work?

She twisted the *wires* back into the *nuts,* while Rez gazed in wonder at the image frozen on her phone. "Is this a scrying tool?"

"It's a phone," Heather explained. "I mostly use it to text people and learn how to do things. That's not magic. It's YouTube."

"It looks like a powerful teaching tool," Rez said in awe. "But how does it use electricity without a...path to the place the electricity comes from?"

Heather opened her mouth to explain, then shrugged. "It's complicated." She sat back on her heels. "I think it's done." She put the casing back over the box and plugged it back in.

Nothing happened. She pushed various buttons in dismay, then exclaimed, "The fuse box!"

Vesta raced her to the kitchen and skidded around in circles while Heather opened the fuse box and reset the breaker.

The box grumbled to life, reluctantly started the fan blades and began to spew increasingly cold air.

Rez backed away from it in alarm. "Is it supposed to do that?"

Heather came to stand in front of it fearlessly. "That is exactly what it's supposed to do," she said in relief. Already, the air in the room was considerably more comfortable.

"Now there's at least a chance of being able to sleep tonight," she said in relief. She glanced at him. "I guess you'll need a place to stay."

Rez hated to ask her for anything, even as his suspicion that she was deliberately enticing him for nefarious purposes faded to nothing. "I do not wish to impose," he said reluctantly.

Heather waved a careless hand. "I've got an air

mattress, you can sleep out here on the floor. I promise not to peek. Not that I haven't already...ah, never mind."

If she had intended to seduce him, it was doubtful that she would offer him private space. Rez didn't understand her motives, or *her*, or even the world he found himself in, but he was ready to accept that she was not malicious.

"I am grateful," Rez said formally. "I will repay your generosity when I am able."

"We can look for your shieldmates tomorrow," Heather suggested. "Maybe they were trapped in ornaments, too. I can check our database at The Ornament Shoppe, and contact some of our ornament dealers. I'll let Fred and Angie know what to look for, too. Are you hungry?"

Rez recognized that he was, beneath his consuming desire for her. "I confess that I am quite ravenous."

"Me, too. I've got some leftover Chinese food and half a rotisserie chicken, if you don't mind some odds and ends."

They left the not-magic cold-making box and she showed him an also-not-magic box that turned cold food from her large cold-making container into steaming, hot food. "Does all of technology focus on changing the temperature of things?" Rez asked, carefully tasting his curious food.

"No," Heather chuckled. "We also have a lot of technology invested in moving people and things from place to place, and in entertainment."

She showed him pictures of *cars* and *trains* as they ate, and briefly turned on the *television*, which was like a portal or a scrying glass, but offered no actual interaction, only a selection of plays and loud opinions. "This requires more context than you have, I'm afraid." She turned it off and Rez was grateful because it all seemed like a great deal to absorb and his head already felt uncomfortably full.

The food was strange, but nourishing and unobjection-able. Heather let him carry their dishes to the sink, and load them into another not-magic box that would clean them.

"This must all be really strange to you," she said to him with sympathy as she unfolded a flexible, rubbery cloth and began to blow it up with a foot pump.

"Strange does not begin to cover it," Rez admitted. "I am…grateful for your patience and your hospitality."

"I'd probably be just as lost in your world," Heather said gently.

"Is this…is this a good world?" Rez asked.

Heather stopped blowing up the air mattress and looked at him in consternation. "How do you judge some-thing like that?" she asked. "I mean, this world has its flaws, and its problems, and its drunk jerks. But…it also has music that will heal your soul, and beautiful art, and unselfish people doing amazing things. It's a *complicated* world. And…yeah, I think it's a *good* world at the end of the day."

Rez lowered his head. "That is…comforting," he said quietly. "The world I left no longer had those things. It was once a place of light and beauty, but a darkness came and tainted our magic. The crown was broken and we were the final hope to restore it." A final hope that had failed, Rez realized.

"That's terrible," Heather murmured. She resumed the tedious act of filling the mattress with air, then discon-nected the foot pump. "I hope you're comfortable on this," she said apologetically. "If you get hungry, you can have a snack from the fridge. Oh, and let me show you the bathroom."

She demonstrated the shower, and the uncomfortable chair proved to be a clever, water-flushing waste receptacle.

The sink hand-pumps and the shower serpent required no pumping whatsoever, just a gentle adjustment of the handle and clean, clear water in multiple temperatures poured out.

"Don't waste it," Heather cautioned. "I pay utilities here."

She gave him a fresh towel and sheepishly picked up the towel that Vesta had claimed for her own.

Then she left him, closing the door behind her.

Rez could not resist trying again to scry in the unblemished mirror, and this time, he felt like the magic was tangible to his will for a few moments before skittering away. Perhaps time and patience would adjust him to the strange frequencies of this world.

He finished preparing himself for rest and came out to find that there were sheets and luxurious blankets spread out on his temporary bed, complete with thick pillows.

Vesta was already lying in the middle of it, wriggling joyously.

"Come on, sweetie," Heather said.

For one brief moment, Rez thought she meant him, then realized with a pang that she was referring to the little gray dog, who was pointedly ignoring her and wagging her tail slowly.

"Heather of Apartment 35…" Rez wasn't sure how to continue when she turned her eyes to him. "Thank you."

"You're welcome…" She was trembling, almost like her little dog did, and Rez realized that she was standing very close, her head tipped up to him. He could kiss her, he thought achingly. He could sweep her into his arms and lay her down on that bed and lose himself for a little while with her.

He could not blame that desire on her or on magic she

claimed she didn't have. It was entirely him, craving entirely her.

"Good night," she said faintly, and she backed all the way down the hallway.

She was stepping sideways into her bed chamber before Vesta realized that she was being abandoned. She scrambled off the temporary bed and flew after her mistress.

Rez wished he could do the same.

CHAPTER 8

*H*eather didn't sleep well, and woke frequently to wonder if she'd gone stark raving mad the day before. Fae knights trapped in glass ornaments seemed highly unlikely when she was alone in her bed at night with the door shut.

Heat hallucination?

Sheer desperation?

Too much reading before bed?

She'd been looking through her college mythology texts just a few weeks ago, thumbing through the color plates, wistfully wondering if knights in shining armor ever really existed as she looked for ideas for new Renaissance Fair garb.

Had she manifested her buried desires by accident, or would she wake up the next morning to find her apartment empty?

She thought over everything that Rez had said and done, and found that remembering what he looked like, how he smelled, how warm his skin was, was more than enough to keep her from further sleep.

After a while, sighing at the hours left before the alarm went off, Heather turned on her bedside lamp and leaned over the side of the bed for her second knitting bag.

Her first knitting bag was out in the living room, where a magical unicorn knight may or may not be sleeping on her floor. This bag was a project she hadn't touched for a while, and it took a moment of staring at the needles to remember where she was on it.

Her first few purls were halting, and she had to undo several stitches before she found her rhythm. Then Heather sighed back against her pillows and found the comfort that she always dredged up when she was knitting.

Clack, clack.

Clackclack…

She could focus on the pattern, on the design that was woven with every row. Vesta turned over on the bed next to her and slept for a while with all four legs pointing into the air.

Clack.

Clack.

Clackclack. Clack.

Clack.

The yarn tamed to her needles, and she was able, for a moment, to turn chaos into contentment.

It wasn't long before she heard stirring from the living room. The steps were quiet, but heavy, and she knew she wasn't imagining things when the toilet flushed the way she had showed Rez the night before.

It flushed again.

And then flushed again, gargling.

Heather got up and pulled on her clothes, Vesta grumbling at being disturbed, then cautiously opened the bedroom door. She could see down the hallway to the air mattress on the floor, sheets rumpled invitingly.

She hesitated, then knocked on the bathroom door. "Everything okay in there?"

Rez pulled the door open swiftly. "I apologize," he said. "You said not to waste utilities, but I had never seen such a device in action. I...er...appear to have broken it in my enthusiasm."

He was wearing only the pants that he'd been wearing the night before, his bare chest everything that Heather remembered. For a moment, it rendered her speechless, then she ran out of air and had to breathe again.

"No, it's okay, you just didn't give the bowl enough time to fill up again," Heather said, trying to sound as if he hadn't made her tongue long for something else to do than talk. The toilet fill gave its last hiss. "It will work fine again now."

Rez, from cautious arm's length, flushed it again, and his face lit up to see it work properly.

"Fascinating," he exclaimed.

Heather laughed nervously. "Are you hungry?"

The glance he gave her suggested he wasn't thinking of food. "I am."

"Cereal okay?"

"What is *cereal okay?*" Rez asked curiously.

"I'll show you," Heather squeaked.

Vesta came wandering hopefully from the bedroom at the sound of food in the kitchen, and she had apparently forgotten that Rez was visiting, because she gave a startled bark, and then scampered for the greeting she thought she was due.

Rez approved of Heather's sugar-frosted wheat squares, and downed a second bowl when she offered it.

"We need to get you some more clothing today," Heather said firmly, working very hard at not staring at his chest as she put her dishes in the dishwasher. "And today I have dinner at my mother's. I work weekends, and because I can't make it to Sunday dinners, we always get together on the last Friday of the month." After agonizing over whether to leave Rez alone in her apartment, cast him loose on the outside world, or bring him with her, Heather had realized that she didn't have a choice. "You're coming with me."

"I would be honored to meet your family," Rez said politely. He didn't seem to feel that implied anything, to Heather's gratitude, but she knew that her mother would assume differently.

"Let's shower and we'll catch the eleven o'clock bus."

Rez looked at her blankly, and she set him up with the shower.

Listening to him shower was almost as bad as watching him slink around her apartment without a shirt, because Heather could picture everything he was doing, and she had a very clear memory of certain attributes she'd gotten an eyeful of the day before.

She was grateful to switch places with him, and her own shower was on the chilly side by design.

It was with extreme reluctance that Heather led Rez out of her apartment and dead-bolted the door behind her. "It's really important to lock up in this neighborhood," she pointed out when he puzzled over her action. "I don't know about where you come from, but we can't just leave things unguarded."

"That seems sensible," Rez said agreeably.

His reaction to motor vehicles was exactly as Heather had anticipated, and even though she had shown him photographs, he was clearly alarmed by their size and speed, and fascinated by their styling.

"Stay on the sidewalk," she cautioned him when he

started to wander. "Cars are only supposed to drive on the road."

She pointed out the lines and traffic signals, and led him to the bus stop as she tried to fill him in on how to greet people and navigate.

A panhandler shuffled towards them with an outstretched hand.

"I shake his hand?" Rez confirmed.

"No, no," Heather hastened to stop him. "He's asking for money." To the panhandler, in a discouraging tone, "Nothing today."

"Screw you, lady," the man snarled, but he eyed Rez cautiously and wandered down the street towards the next stop.

"He was disrespectful," Rez said disapprovingly.

"He's not all there in the head," Heather said. "You can't take it personally."

As they sat at the bus stop, she told him the backstory they would use with her mother.

"We are going there now, in one of these cars?" Rez asked, gesturing to one of the vans that drove past.

"We are going to BigMart first, in a bus. Ah, there's our line."

Heather rose from the hard bench and pulled Rez up with her to the edge of the sidewalk. She could feel his hesitation and resolve as the bus, which must be absolutely monstrous to someone who had never seen one, pulled up in front of them. They waited for the people to come out, then Heather led him up into the bus. She held their fare out to the surly-looking bus driver and he printed them the round-trip tickets.

"Do I shake his hand?" Rez hissed near her ear.

Heather shook her head and led him back to the seats. He gingerly sat beside her, and jolted back to his feet when the hydraulics hissed, the doors shut, and the bus began it's winding ramble towards the city.

"This is *amazing,*" Rez said too loudly, plastering himself to the window.

Heather was keenly aware of the attention they were getting. Even dressed in ill-fitting clothes, Rez was a lot of man, and he was loud and amazed enough that they were the object of many suspicious glances.

As the bus filled, she shushed him, and they moved closer together to let a woman with a heavy armload of groceries take the seat beside them.

She had to stand up to let them out at her stop, and Rez gave her a bow of his head. "Your bounty is great," he said admiringly.

The woman stared at them like they'd escaped a loony bin.

"Sorry!" Heather exclaimed. "He's...new to this world."

She dragged him off the bus before he could say anything else.

"Is this our destination?" Rez asked, staring.

"Welcome to BigMart," Heather said, dread in her stomach.

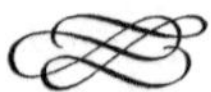

CHAPTER 9

"*D*o I shake *her* hand?" Rez asked as they passed through doors that slipped opened at their approach and a cheerfully smiling woman offered them a flyer.

Heather shook her head at both Rez and the woman and Rez had to wonder if he had misunderstood her instructions about the standard of greeting.

He followed her into a market so large and wonderful that he had to stand a moment and gape.

To one side stretched edible goods, great bins of fruits and vegetables, some of them recognizable, some of them things he'd never seen before. They were in all the rainbow colors, wrapped in thin plastic, tied with colored strings, spilling out of boxes. There were glazed cases showing steaming dishes and cold cream salads and meat sliced impossibly thin. Beyond he caught sight of heaping shelves of bread and rolls, neatly stacked.

To the other side, as if that was not miraculous enough, were racks and racks of clothing goods. Perfect duplicates of shirts and pants were hung in tidy rows.

There were stacks of absolutely identical trousers, and bins of socks and even shoes.

"Where are the sellers?" he asked, when he finally realized one of the reasons it all seemed so odd.

"The...what?" Heather had walked several steps away before she realized he wasn't beside her.

"The sellers," Rez repeated. "Shouldn't the seller of the fruit be beside her bin? How do you pay? Do you not have hawkers?"

"This is all one store," Heather explained, gesturing wide. "One person...er...company owns the whole thing. There are some helpers—there's one in that blue shirt. But you just wander the whole place and fill up...over here. This is a shopping cart."

Rez eyed the wheeled contraption with some trepidation, swiftly concluding that it was a method of transporting goods. It boggled his mind that a person could purchase enough to need wheeled conveyance, but when Heather put it front of him, he pushed it obediently after her.

She ignored the fantastic food and took him towards the back of the store, into an area that he recognized by the false models as men's clothing.

Here, again, were racks and racks of identical garments. But no, they weren't identical. Heather dug through them, looking at tiny parchments attached to the cloth. They were different *sizes*.

"This might fit you," she said, holding up an oddly fashioned shirt with buttons all down the front. "Let's try it on."

Rez began to strip off his ill-fitting shirt and Heather gave a squeak of alarm. "No, you can't undress here."

Rez froze, his shirt already mostly off. "It is unseemly?"

"Really unseemly." Heather appeared to have trouble

breathing and Rez took a certain amount of pride from being able to fluster her. "They have dressing rooms. But let's pick a few more things first."

They loaded the cart with beige and blue trousers and t-shirts. Wrapped packages of socks and undergarments were added. "Don't try those on," Heather cautioned. "We just have to guess on those."

A few pairs of shoes were thrown in, fascinating squishy things emblazoned with bright colors. One of them squeaked and after Rez tested the mechanism a few times, Heather put them back on the shelf.

She showed him to the dressing rooms, and he obediently tried every item on, modeling each one in turn.

They narrowed the selection down considerably.

"Do we consult with a tailor now?" Rez asked.

"A tailor?" Heather asked.

"To refine the fit?"

She blinked at him. "Don't they fit?"

Had he insulted her? "They will do," he said contritely.

"Do you really have everything fitted to you personally?" Heather asked in astonishment.

"Are all of your people the same shape?" Rez asked, confused. He had certainly observed people in all forms and sizes.

Heather was fingering one of the shirts thoughtfully. "Not even close. I guess that most people don't know how to sew, and a tailor seems like an extravagance if the clothing is close enough."

"It will clothe me," Rez assured her. "Even if it does not truly flatter me."

Heather grinned at him. "You're a little vain, you know?"

Rez's consternation must have been apparent on his

face, because she swiftly added, "Don't feel bad. It's nice to see that you aren't a complete unicorn."

Consternation turned back to confusion. "I...*am* a unicorn."

"We call something absolutely perfect and unattainable a *unicorn*," Heather explained. "Because it will never happen, everyone has flaws. And...unicorns are impossible."

"I am not impossible," Rez said quietly.

"Sometimes, I think you are," she replied.

CHAPTER 10

I really did get a unicorn, Heather thought.

He was so hot that people gave him a double-take in the BigMart, and he was unfailingly kind and courteous. He shook hands with one of the stockers before Heather could stop him, to the poor kid's complete confusion, and Heather thought that she should probably explain the use of the gesture a little better.

She took him to the toiletries aisle next. "I don't know if you want to use my shampoo or not, but I'm pretty sure my deodorant won't suit you."

"Deodorant?"

"It's July in Georgia. Deodorant is one of those things that is necessary to maintain our...er...social covenant not to stink too badly."

Rez dutifully smelled the tubes that she uncapped for him, and expressed delight in each of them. "Is it...very dear?" he asked. "Perfumes in my world are rather rare and expensive."

Heather started pointing out the prices. "This is quite cheap."

Rez frowned at the cart and fingered some of the tags. "I fear you are spending a great deal on me. The vehicle of transportation also took your coins."

"Tips at the Ren Faire have been good lately, and I had some extra money socked away for a rainy day," Heather said quickly. "And..." She came to a stop, looking away as if the manly body wash in front of her was suddenly fascinating.

It was hard to put her finger on the connection that she felt for Rez, hard to define how she could no more leave him to fend for himself than she could have abandoned Vesta. He needed her, and she hadn't thought twice about making sure he had a few basic things. "It's not like I'm buying you top-end anything," she ended lamely.

"I will find a way to repay you," he vowed.

"It doesn't have to be like that," Heather said, turning back to look at him. "We call it paying it forward. Some-time in your life, everyone needs help. So when you have a chance to help someone, you do, and when they have a chance to help someone else, they do. And when you need help, hopefully someone will help you. It isn't...an exchange of services. It's doing the right thing when you have the means."

Rez was quiet. "You were correct," he said thoughtfully.

"I was? About what?"

"This is a *good* world."

Heather couldn't define the tightness in her chest.

Fortunately, Rez spotted the shaving tools on the oppo-site side of the aisle. "Are these for the shaving of beards?" He ran a hand over the stubble that only made him hotter.

"Ah no," Heather said. "Those are for ladies. Men's are over here."

"What is the difference?"

"Price, mostly," Heather said wryly. "And yours don't come in pink."

"That is a shame," Rez said with regret that could not have been faked.

Heather giggled.

They selected a few more key items, Rez accidentally sprayed shaving cream on his nose as he inspected the canister, and Heather turned the shopping cart to the checkout line.

"You look reluctant," Rez observed, wiping the cream from his perfect nose. "Is it too much to buy?"

"No, nothing like that," Heather said warmly. "It's just time to go see my mother."

"This makes you nervous?" Rez guessed.

"You have no idea."

CHAPTER 11

$\mathcal{R}$ez was on pins and needles by the time they arrived on foot at a modest cottage in a neighborhood of similar buildings. There was a spread of unnaturally short grass before it, which seemed common for this world, and an ineffective looking fence. An odd wooden sentinel with a shuttered metal box at the top stood near the gate.

"It's a mailbox," Heather explained shortly as she ushered him along the short path to the front door. "Try...not to stare at stuff. Pretend to be the strong, silent type, and I'll do my best to keep you caught up." She paused at the door before knocking and adjusted the collar of his new shirt. "Do you remember your backstory?"

They had rehearsed their fiction on the bus ride over. "I am a foreign exchange student from Morocco studying medieval literature at Georgia Tech. I did not have a place to stay when the dorms closed for summer and I am *couch surfing*. We met at the *Ren Faire* where you work. If your mother asks my religion, I am *Catholic*."

"I'll try to steer clear of those topics, but we'll see."

She looked as nervous as Rez felt, and Vesta was trembling in her arms, but she lifted her chin and turned to the door, giving it a firm, loud knock before she opened it and walked in. "Mama! We're here!"

"In here, sweetie!" came the warm reply, and Rez followed Heather into a house filled with *smells*.

"I hope you're hungry," Heather said, putting Vesta down.

If Rez had not been, the tantalizing scents would have ensured his appetite. "What amazing dish has been prepared?" he asked as he stepped into the kitchen, completely forgetting his intention to remain silent.

The woman who emerged from behind a refrigerator door gave him a wide-eyed look of astonishment. "When you said you were bringing a man, I didn't realize you meant you were bringing that much man. Heather Rose, have you been holding out on your mother?"

"Yeah, Heather, have you been holding out?" An adolescent version of Heather appeared in the far doorway, chewing something in her mouth.

"My sister, Charlotte," Heather introduced with a sigh. "My mother. This is Rez. Is Fiona here?"

"No," Charlotte said with a careless slouch. "She's out with her heathen doctor tonight."

"Charlotte Ann," their mother said warningly. "We got company."

"Is this guy a heathen? Or a doctor?" Charlotte was clearly unimpressed by the use of her full title or the warning in her mother's voice.

"I am a foreign exchange student," Rez offered. Was he supposed to shake her hand? He was thoroughly unsure.

"Juicy," Charlotte replied, and their mother swatted a towel in her direction.

"Dinner is in ten minutes. Haven't you got something to do?"

"Yup," Charlotte said, and she disappeared out the door she'd come in.

"What's for supper?" Heather asked cautiously.

"Fried chicken, mac n cheese, candied yams, collard greens, and how long have you been *friends*?"

Heather had been slipping a carrot off of a plate of vegetable pieces, and she dropped it on the floor. Vesta was on it in a moment.

"No!" Heather protested to both her mother and her dog. "He's just crashing on my floor for a while, Mama. Drop it, Vesta. Drop it!"

Vesta fled with her prize, and hid beneath the table. Heather crouched down to wrest the carrot from her and her mother gave Rez a long, considering look. "You a Methodist?" she asked suspiciously.

Rez dredged his memory. "I am couch surfing," he said desperately. "We met at the Ren Faire. I am Catholic." By habit, he ended with, "My lady."

She sniffed in reply. "Could be worse," she said grudgingly. "You can call me June. Or Mama June, I see you suffering."

Something began to claxon violently, and Rez automatically reached for a sword he didn't have. "Biscuits," Heather's mother said, turning it off and reaching for heavy mittens. A door in one of her technology boxes opened with steaming heat and she removed a hot sheet of baked nuggets on it.

"Can we set the table for you, Mama?" Heather asked, standing triumphant with her half-gnawed carrot.

"Bless you, yes. Your sister's good for nothing at this age."

Heather dragged Rez into the next room, and handed

him a pile of placemats. He ordered them around the table while she collected silverware and then showed him how to lay it out, naming each utensil as she went.

"I do know forks and spoons," Rez said, wondering if he should feel insulted. "Your knives are very dull."

Then the food began to appear. There were baskets of biscuits, piles of fried fowl legs, a steaming, creamy dish covered in cheese, a bowl of dark, leafy greens, a plate of vegetables, a small dish of round dark fruits in some kind of brine, and a bowl of small yellow kernels in cream sprinkled with green herbs. Great pats of rich butter were added to the table, and dark and white spices in glass jars with holes in the lid.

Rez stared in wonder. He had suspected that Heather's world was rich, but now he wasn't sure if he'd ever been in a land so fortunate. "This is magnificent," he told Heather's mother honestly. "Your generosity is great."

She looked pleased, and pointed him to the seat next to her. "Call your sister," she told Heather.

Heather went to the doorway and hollered, "Charlotte!"

"Lord, sweetie, I could have done that myself," Mama said crossly.

Rez knew that Heather didn't want to risk leaving him alone with her mother and appreciated her care.

Charlotte came slouching to the table and took a seat across from Rez. He eyed the food, but paused when no one else reached for it. They were clearly waiting for something.

Mama took the seat at the head of the table and folded her hands before her. She closed her eyes and bowed her head. Rez followed suit as Heather and Charlotte did, keeping his eyes to slits so he could observe the ritual.

"Jesus, we ask that you bless this food you've graciously

given us, and ask you look over our family and our new friends, and keep Charlotte from rolling her eyes during prayer in Jesus' name, Amen."

Charlotte and Heather both murmured, "Amen," and Rez did the same.

"Now eat," Mama said.

And he did.

CHAPTER 12

Heather gradually relaxed through the meal. She had forgotten that the one sure way to gain her mother's approval was to enjoy her food, and Rez did so with the earnest dedication of a man who had been starved for years.

There were prying questions during the meal, but far less than Heather expected, and they were all harmlessly deflected with more appreciation for the offerings on the table. Charlotte offered snarky observations and picked at her food while their mother chided her half-heartedly for ingratitude.

Rez's plate was heaped with gnawed chicken bones by the time that Charlotte grudgingly gathered their plates.

"I made caramel cake," Mama said as she stood.

Heather groaned. "I could not stuff in another bite, Mama. Have mercy."

"Mercy is children who respect their mother," she complained in return. "Rez, would *you* like a slice of my caramel cake?"

"I do not know what that is, Mama June," Rez said honestly.

"Oh, *honey!*" Sometimes Heather thought her mother should have been an actress instead of a dental hygienist. "Oh, honey, that's *tragic*. Well, I guarantee they haven't got anything like my caramel cake in that Morocco. Let me get you a slice."

"I have enjoyed this meal enormously," Rez told Heather as Mama left. "How do I reward her for this? Do we pay, as with the transportation?"

"Pay? Not on your life. That would insult her. All you do is appreciate it and eat yourself comatose. That's what family meals here are like."

Rez seemed to approve of that, and also of the layered caramel cake that appeared in front of him.

Heather was forced to eat her own slice as well, lamenting that she wasn't going to be able to lace up her Ren Faire garb. "Where are you putting it?" she asked Rez. "I didn't think there was room in those pants for anything else."

When she heard her own words, her ears lit up with heat, Charlotte spit crumbs on the table laughing, and Mama scolded her.

After they cleared up, Heather offered to wash the dishes, and Rez swiftly added his willingness to help her. "You can dry," Heather said, stacking the dessert plates. Mama retired to the living room to work on her knitting and Charlotte disappeared. Vesta was snoring on the couch, full from all the scraps she'd been fed.

Alone with Rez again, Heather was keenly aware of his magnetic *presence*, of the solid mass of him as he delicately dried plates. The kitchen was small, and they accidentally brushed against each other several times as she pointed out where and how to put the dishes away.

"Oops," Heather said, dropping a clump of bubbles on his foot as she jerked back from his touch.

Charlotte had the terrible timing to come in just then, but she ignored them to go to the door and peer out at Mama. When she turned back, Heather and Rez were as far apart in the kitchen as they could manage and she eyed them suspiciously.

"Mama's got a boyfriend," she announced, and Heather nearly dropped her plate.

"What do you mean, she's got a boyfriend?" Heather hissed. That *would* explain why Mama hadn't been quite as nosy as she'd expected. "Who is it?"

"The guy at the printing shop who's been doing the church bulletins. He's started attending church with us on Sundays, and I caught him leaving the house at *three* yesterday morning." Charlotte looked positively triumphant.

"Mr. Wright from Print Co? He's so..."

"White?" Charlotte guessed.

"I was going to say bald. Is it serious?" Heather asked. Bubbles were drying on the plate she was holding and she turned to rinse them off. Was nothing in her life sacred? First naked fae knights appeared in her apartment, and now her mother was *dating*?

"He's going to the Good Book Club with her," Charlotte said smugly.

It *was* serious.

Heather turned to wash another plate, keenly aware of Rez's regard.

"I take it this is an alarming turn of events?" he said gently.

"Mama raised the three of us alone after Dad died. I guess I'm just surprised. I'm...glad for her."

"It isn't easy...to be alone."

Heather looked up into his earnest face, all her breath sucked away.

Charlotte cleared her throat uncomfortably. "Speaking of awkward," she said, and then she retreated back to her room.

"I like your family," Rez said, almost shyly. "The closest to family I have—had—were my shieldmates."

"We'll start looking for them," Heather promised. "Soon." She considered. "Could you…wait here a sec?"

"I can finish these dishes," Rez said with a nod.

Heather dried her hands on a towel and went out into the living room.

The television was on, but turned down low, and the comfortable clack, clack, clack of Mama's knitting made everything feel perfectly normal for the first time in days.

But everything *wasn't* normal. Everything was as far from normal as Heather had ever imagined it *could* be.

"Guess Charlotte told you about Mr. Wright," Mama said.

"You could have invited him for dinner," Heather said. She picked up Vesta and curled up at the other end of the couch with her feet underneath her. It was a familiar place, safe and happy. She and Mama had learned to knit together on this very couch when she was Charlotte's age, and it had gotten them through a lot of tough conversations.

"Wasn't sure how you'd feel about that," Mama confessed, and Heather felt a little like the world was upside down.

"I'd like it," she said softly. "Mama, you deserve a nice guy who makes you happy. I guess I just never thought you...wanted one."

"I never did," Mama said. "I had you girls to keep me

company, and church to keep me busy. I wasn't looking, and I never expected it."

She continued to look at her knitting, as if she had to watch her fingers even though Heather knew she didn't.

"Why Mr. Wright?" Heather asked reluctantly.

"Why not, honey? He's a good man with a good heart and a great ass."

"Mama!" Heather had to bury her laughter into one of the couch pillows.

"Speaking of great asses..."

"We're not like that, Mama, I swear. He's just staying on my floor for a while."

That caused her to stop knitting. "I saw the way you look at each other," she said severely. "And you brought him to dinner."

"He didn't have anywhere else to go," Heather protested.

Mama gave a skeptical snort and resumed her winding and clacking. "Say what you will, honey."

For a moment, they sat quietly together, then both spoke at once: "It's okay."

They laughed, and Mama repeated herself. "It's okay, Heather. I know that times aren't like they were, and if you found someone that makes you happy, that's a blessing."

Heather's chest felt several sizes too small. "We just met," she said quietly.

"Sometimes, you just know," Mama said firmly.

Heather held Vesta too close and the dog wriggled for freedom, bouncing off the couch to return to the kitchen and lick the floor as soon as she was released.

"You, too, Mama," Heather said at last. "I mean, it's okay. You should invite Mr. Wright for dinner next time."

Whatever she might have answered was cut short by a

tremendous crash from the kitchen and Vesta raced out with her tail between her legs, shaking in fear.

"Forgive me," Rez greeted her at the kitchen door. "I thought I might sharpen some knives, and I fear I have damaged your drawer." Cutlery was spread across the kitchen floor. Charlotte had appeared at the far door and she scowled at everyone.

"Goodness gracious," Mama said. "You didn't break anything. It just falls out if you pull it too far. You two get this picked up, now."

Charlotte vanished, as if she smelled chores.

Heather and Rez picked up the silverware and reassembled the drawer as Mama went back to her television and knitting. Heather caught herself watching Rez out of the corner of her eye, thoughtful and cautiously excited.

It wasn't just that he was an eyeful of candy, as if he'd stepped fully assembled from her sweatiest fantasies. It wasn't just that he was interesting and hopelessly lost in her world. Heather had dated *unique* guys before, and that was usually their only positive quality.

But Rez was sweet, too, and polite, and brave. She couldn't help remembering how he'd snarled at Marcus over the landlord's rudeness, how he'd boarded a giant roaring bus because Heather said it was safe, even though he was clearly dubious. When he listened, Heather felt like he was *really* listening, not just impatiently waiting for his chance to talk.

That, and the sight of him set her body on fire.

Sometimes, you just know.

Heather found the last spoon under the kitchen sink and showed Rez how to put the drawer back into the slot.

"I'm sorry for the disruption," Rez said mournfully, and Heather's heart thawed a little more.

"It's fine," she said, thinking about his larger disruption

in her staid little life. She was standing very close to him, and she wondered if she was brave enough to kiss him in her mother's kitchen. "It's fine. I'm glad."

She *wasn't* that brave.

"Glad?" Rez asked, puzzled.

"Never mind," Heather said, smiling up at him. "The last bus back is at seven, so we should get going."

CHAPTER 13

*R*ez woke early the following morning in Heather's strange quarters, and stared at the ceiling a long time.

He didn't understand why he missed the feeling of having her in his arms. How could he *miss* something he'd never had? He missed his shieldmates, and a world where things made sense, and his sword, as he should. But somehow, he also missed Heather. Had he dreamed of her?

From the bedroom down the hall came a sound of beeping, a muffled curse, and a muted thump.

After a few moments, Heather emerged from the bedroom. Vesta followed her slowly, yawning and stretching each leg one at a time.

"Rise and shine, Lancelot," Heather said, stumbling into the bathroom. "We're going to the Ren Faire this morning."

Rez obediently rose, but wasn't entirely certain how to shine, so he settled for getting out the cereal supplies as he'd seen her do the morning before.

"This is nice," she said in gratitude and surprise when

she emerged after a brief shower dressed completely differently than anything else he'd seen her in. She wore a lightweight underdress with a kirtle laced over it, and she had a cloth over her hair.

They ate together, and Heather halting explained her job.

"I work as a period re-enactor," she said. "I do spinning demonstrations and sell handcrafted wool."

"Is there another kind of wool?" Rez asked.

"Well, it *can* be made in a factory," Heather said.

"Does wool not grow on sheep here?"

Heather rubbed her face. "Well, wool does, usually, but there are other kinds of yarn, acrylic and you know what, that's not really the point. I've got a job that I do at the Ren Faire, and I'll need to do it, and *your* job will be to stay quiet and blend in. I think you'll be really good at this. We're going to borrow some garb from Allen, and all you have to do is be yourself."

"I am better at being myself than other people," Rez told her gravely. He loved the way her eyes crinkled with humor.

"You're going to do fine," she assured him.

He wasn't as sure, particularly when her friend's car pulled up in front of the apartment building.

"Thanks again!" Heather said, as they bent, one after another, to sit on the tiny bench in the battered-looking vehicle. "Allen, this is Rez. Rez, this is Allen. Allen runs the booth next to the fiber tent I work in. Rez is going to be helping me out today."

"Nice to meet you!" Allen said jovially. "Buckle up!"

Heather pulled a harness from the side of the car and attached it over herself. Rez glanced back and found a similar device on his side. He figured out how to seamlessly pull it out after a few tries, and Heather reached over to show him to fasten it into place.

The car ride was significantly different than a bus ride had been. It was harder to see things, and Rez felt uncomfortably *stuck*. It didn't help that he had to fold himself into the narrow space, his knees jammed against the seat before him.

When they arrived at their destination, Allen made the machine stop roaring and opened his door. Heather got out on her own side, and Rez opened his door in the same fashion as she had, with a lever, but he was drawn back by the harness that was still constraining him when he tried to escape.

He tugged at the buckle but was unsuccessful in unlatching it. He was able to pull the straps loose enough that he could slip out underneath them, with some difficulty, and Allen was staring at him curiously as he made the final extraction. "My thanks for your conveyance," he said with as much dignity as he could muster.

"Method actor?" Allen guessed.

Rez had no idea what that was, so he grinned and shrugged, which seemed to be a suitable reply.

Allen handed him a bag. "Here's some garb that should fit you."

Heather led them through a gate, showing her badge for passage, and took him to a facility like her bathroom, but with many stalls.

When he emerged, her gaze was approving and rather warmer than it had been when he went in.

"Yes, that will do just *fine*," she agreed with Allen.

It was considerably more comfortable than the clothing she had bought him at the BigMart, more familiar in shape and style.

"My lord," Allen said, bowing.

Rez automatically returned the gesture.

They walked down dusty aisles of a faire that was just beginning to awaken. Merchants were opening tents and uncovering wares.

Rez was awed by the quality of the merchandise. There was delicate pottery and clothing of such fine weave and stitching that he had to look to find the tiny threads. There were blown glass figures that gave him pause, remembering the ornament he'd been imprisoned in, and he searched in vain for something that might be one of his shieldmates.

Allen went ahead of them while he lingered with Heather, and by the time they arrived at his tent, he had opened up the front of his tent.

Rez spotted Allen's wares and his eyes lit up. "You are a blacksmith?" he observed. "I am Rez, knight of the realm, defender of the fallen kingdom. I am sorely in need of a sword."

Allen grinned. "My lord, I had no idea!" He bowed extravagantly. "I am humbly at your service, sir knight. I pray my tools find your favor."

Rez was already lifting one of the largest swords from the display and sweeping it into the air. "What folly is this?" he demanded.

"Folly?" Allen said, his grin faltering.

Rez stepped through a series of steps and swipes, disappointment blooming in his chest.

A small crowd of people stopped to stare, and when he had executed a particularly fast series of moves, they applauded.

"This is a child's blade," Rez said in disgust. "It is poorly forged and too slight to withstand the weakest attack. It is badly balanced and will hold no edge."

Allen gave Heather a disbelieving look.

Rez took a threatening step towards him. "Are you a charlatan, selling substandard weapons that will risk a man's life in battle? Do you profit from the failure of your tools?"

"Wait, wait," Heather said swiftly. "Rez, put the sword down. No, he's not trying to cheat anyone, those aren't meant to be used in battle."

Rez stopped, but did not lower his blade. "What is a sword for, if not for battle?" Every time he started to feel comfortable in this world, it seemed to be more strange than ever.

"It's just for show," Heather said, rushing forward to pull Rez away from Allen. "Sorry, Allen, he's…ah…taking things a little too seriously."

Allen took the sword back with a scowl, and they parted with suspicious glares at each other as the people watching gradually dispersed.

Heather took Rez to the tent next door and had him help her take down the front panel. There was a spinning wheel and many shelves of both wool and yarn, as well as several examples of woven clothing. Heather showed him to the back of the tent, where a small private area was open to the sweltering sky above.

"Are you hungry?" she asked. "Let's go get some food before the faire actually opens."

CHAPTER 14

"You know," Heather said regretfully, "I probably didn't pick the best ways to introduce you to my world." She was nibbling on a roasted turkey leg as she leaned against the railing to the competition ring. Vesta was sitting at her feet, whining occasionally to remind them of how hungry and neglected she was.

Rez, shifting the borrowed tabard on his shoulders, shot her a questioning look. "In what way, lady?"

"This," Heather said, spreading her fingers to indicate the festive Faire, banners waving over colorful tents. "This isn't how we really live. This is play-acting. It's something we do for entertainment. We don't eat this food or wear these clothes."

"And yet we are eating this food and wearing these clothes," Rez pointed out.

"But it's not *normal*," Heather insisted. "I should probably be introducing you to fast food and television and...I don't know, American sports? You're seeing kind of a niche group of people obsessing about a really obscure hobby here."

Rez considered. "It is a little...uneasy," he admitted. "It is familiar, more familiar than the other things you have shared with me. But it is also different."

"Uncanny valley," Heather told him. "When something is similar to something you know, but just the wrong amount of different, you sometimes feel ill at ease. It's worse than something being *really* off. We call this the uncanny valley. What's strangest about things here?"

Rez looked around. "The people are happier, more generous. The food is better. The air is sweeter. But I can see how things here are false, like your friend Allen's swords. These tents are not designed to withstand much weather or wear. Everyone's clothing is bright, all of it looks new, unused. Even the people pretending to be poor are fat and clean."

They were standing near the fighting ring. Two heavily-armored men were sparring with large swords, grunting and shouting insults at each other. A small audience was watching from the stands.

"These warriors seem incompetent," Rez said disparagingly. "They would not survive long on a real battlefield with that technique."

Someone beside them laughed and Heather turned to find a familiar face.

"I intended no insult," Rez said swiftly, clearly taking stock of the new man's light armor. He frowned at the wooden sword Levi was holding.

"None taken," Levi said graciously. "They are indeed poor specimens."

"Hi, Levi," Heather said. "This is Rez. He's...from way out of town."

Rez bowed his head courteously. "It is my pleasure to meet another friend of Heather of Apartment 35's."

Levi gave him an appraising look. "You consider yourself a warrior of some skill, I take it?"

"I don't know, Levi…" Heather started to say.

"I am one of the finest fighters in…in Way Out of Town," Rez said, beginning to smile. It looked just a little bloodthirsty.

"This is a bad idea," Heather said firmly.

"I'll go easy on him," Levi promised her, though it wasn't Rez she was actually worried about. "He's a big guy, but you know what they say about big guys and how they fall."

"Don't make me beat the two of you apart with my turkey leg," Heather said smartly. "A fight between you two is probably the worst idea I've heard in a week. And this was a week where I took a guy I just met to dinner with my *mother*."

"If you disapprove…" Rez said reluctantly.

"You would let your lady keep you from a proper battle?" Levi teased.

"Of course," Rez said courteously.

Heather tried to smother her delight in that response.

"Hide behind Lady Heather's skirts, then," Levi said, raising his voice. "If you are too much a coward to face me yourself."

"Oh, Levi," Heather said pityingly. "You have no idea."

"I am not a coward," Rez said darkly.

"No, of course you're not," Heather told him kindly, bending to feed Vesta a piece from her turkey leg.

"You're just a milksop, tied to your lady's apron strings," Levi said dismissively.

"Levi," Heather said warningly.

Vesta came to Rez's feet, clearly hoping for some of his food, and he knelt to give her the last scrap of his meat, turning his back on Levi.

"You have not even a proper *hound*," Levi scoffed as Vesta gulped down the treat greedily. "My Great Dane leaves shits of greater mass and intelligence."

Stroking Vesta's tiny head, Rez raised his gaze to Heather.

She sighed.

"Try not to hurt him," she said warningly.

"If I damage him, I will endeavor to also heal his wounds," Rez promised, rising to his feet. Heather thought that there was more to the statement than simply promising to bandage him, some deeper meaning.

"Ah!" Levi said, grinning. "Wilt thou meet me on the field, lover of puny canines?" He called the challenge loudly, and Heather realized that the armored knights were leaving the ring and the audience was craning to see if they would be some new entertainment as the announcer declared a winner over the loudspeaker.

"Oh good lord," Heather said. She tossed the remains of her food into a receptacle and wiped her fingers on a paper napkin before stooping to gather Vesta into her arms.

The booming announcer said, "Do we have a new contender in the field?"

"This man has insulted your knights! Let us find you armor and a weapon, stranger, so that I may school you accordingly!" Levi shouted.

The little audience applauded half-heartedly.

"I need neither," Rez growled.

Levi looked uncertain for a moment. "We've got to

meet safety requirements…" he started to say, but Rez strode ahead of him onto the dusty field.

"Not even a sword?" Levi said plaintively, scrambling after him. "What are you going to fight with?"

Heather followed.

"I will take yours," Rez told him. "What are the rules of your combat and how do you start?"

Levi was clearly reconsidering his bluster as they crossed the field. "No headshots, we're not trying to kill each other. A hit with the sword disables a limb, so you can't use it again. We bow, and the tournament master rings a bell. We battle to a surrender or at the tourney master's judgement."

Rez bowed crisply and cracked his knuckles, standing casually with his feet apart.

"Will you take your lady's favor?" Levi asked for the audience's benefit.

Heather sighed as Rez looked confused and pulled a rose-colored cloth from her belt. "This is a terrible idea," she told Levi, and she handed the cloth to Rez. "Kiss it and tuck it into your belt."

Levi only looked amused as Rez obediently did so.

Heather retreated to the fence, not sure she wanted to watch any of it.

Levi bowed and took a fighting stance, and when the bell rang, sprang forward with his wooden sword.

Rez simply reached up and caught the blow on his forearm, punched forward with his other arm and sent the man staggering backwards with a hit square to his chest.

The audience cheered more enthusiastically and Heather caught her breath.

Rez surged forward, the arm he'd caught the sword on behind him in sporting fashion. He slammed bodily into

Levi and reached with his free arm to pluck the sword from Levi's unresisting hands.

Rez gave the sword a few swings before he tossed it, spinning, up in the air. While it fell, he stepped forward, slapped a stunned Levi across the face with his single hand, and then moved back to catch the practice weapon in the same hand. He extended the blade towards the other man's throat.

Heather wasn't sure she had breathed once the entire time.

"I concede," Levi sputtered in astonishment.

The little crowd went wild and the bell from the tower rang out, signaling the end of the bout.

Rez bowed, and offered the sword hilt-first as the announcer hailed the un-armed stranger as the victor, ad-libbing titles for Rez as he went. "The stranger with the air of danger! The fighter with the pants that are tighter!"

Levi, still gasping, gave a shaky bow in return. "Thou has bested me fairly," he said loudly. He offered a hand and Rez gravely shook it. "You have to show me how to do that," he said more quietly. "Damn."

He was rubbing his chest as Rez walked to Heather.

"I would challenge!" Another voice rang out behind him, but Rez continued towards Heather.

"You have defended my dog's honor," she said to him breathlessly. "If you wanted to fight more of them, I won't stop you."

Rez shook his head. "It is that uncanny valley you spoke of," he said sadly. "Fighting is not sport where I come from, and wooden swords are for children with no control, not grown men of skill. Battles were not fought for honor, or titles, or tournaments, but to hold the darkness at bay a little longer, and we knew that each one might be our last. Our final failure."

"You have nothing to be ashamed of," Heather said fiercely. "You cannot blame yourself for the downfall of an entire kingdom. That's absurd."

"If I don't take the responsibility, who does?" Rez asked.

Heather didn't have an answer for him.

CHAPTER 15

"**I**'m doing spinning demonstrations for the rest of the morning," Heather told him firmly as she released Vesta from her handbag to go curl up in a corner of the tent. "I'm going to need you to stay out of the way and not pick fights with anyone."

"I shall endeavor to keep the peace," Rez said reluctantly, lowering himself into one of the lawn chairs behind their tent. He could not quite resist muttering, "Even if *Allen* was clearly defrauding his buyers…"

After a while, he realized that he could watch Heather through a crack in the back tent wall. She spun her wool and answered questions and walked children through spinning their own short, lumpy pieces of yarn. She talked about dyeing wool and sold skeins of yarn and drop spindles. She was bright and friendly and smart, kind to everyone and never impatient with the questions that even Rez recognized as stupid.

He could watch her forever, he thought. The line of her neck, the soft curls of her hair. The graceful way she moved. The curves of her sweet body laced into the flattering dress that swayed around her. Her hands. The planes of her face.

He would never tire of cataloging her beauty.

"You use a different voice," Rez observed, when she came back to drink from her flask of metal and make sure that he hadn't gotten into more trouble.

"I'm attempting a historical accent," she said. "The whole point of the faire is to pretend that we're in a different place and time. It's all part of the illusion."

"I really am in a different place and time," Rez said mournfully. "I do not believe it is an illusion any more."

Heather stepped closer, as if she wanted to comfort him, but before she could speak, there was the sound of angry yelling out in front of the tent.

"Let me make sure there isn't a problem," she said swiftly. Rez followed her.

Unfortunately, there *was* a problem.

Allen was standing in the lane before her tent, a small cluster of people between him and Heather's tent. He was waving around one of his swords.

"You want to disparage my swords?" Allen roared. "Well, I'll show you how well they work!" His face was twisted in rage.

"I don't know if I've ever seen Allen look so angry. I don't know if I've ever seen *anyone* that angry," Heather observed in astonishment.

"I have," Rez said grimly.

When Allen went wading in to the little crowd of people, sword flashing, the people around him seemed to think it was some kind of show or act...until the first screams started, and people began staggering away holding real bleeding wounds.

He was flailing wildly, so it was easy for people to get away and he wasn't focused enough to cause any real harm. Heather fearlessly picked up one of her drop spindles and held it like a weapon.

"Allen, what are you doing?" she demanded, but Rez knew exactly what was happening and moved to stand in front of her.

"He is *ridden*," he said solemnly.

"Ridden? Wait, *dours*?" Heather demanded. "*Here??*"

"I can purge it," Rez said furiously, and then he reached down into himself and changed.

He was power and strength, grace and glory, pure in color and heart...and he was eye-to-eye with a very surprised Vesta.

He should be making the earth tremble with every hoofbeat, but when Rez gave an experimental stomp, nothing happened.

He was impossibly small, and humiliatingly powerless.

Vesta yipped and danced back in an invitation to play, but no matter his size, Rez had a mission.

He galloped out of the tent, head lowered, sensing the darkness in the milling crowd and trying not to get stepped on. Someone's long, swinging skirt nearly knocked him over, and he had to gather himself and leap with all his strength to clear a bag of merchandise that someone had dropped.

Then he was beneath Allen, who reeked of dour-darkness.

Allen slashed at him with the sword, nearly taking off his own foot. Rez swiveled on his back legs and dodged the clumsy blow, driving his horn into Allen's closest boot.

His horn punctured the leather and stabbed into the foot, just barely into the skin. Rez had a bad moment where he thought he could do no good, then the dour *dissolved* in the face of his power. He could almost hear it scream in defeat as the darkness spread like thinning smoke and vanished.

Allen howled, and then his entire voice seemed to change as he shook his head in confusion, lowering his sword and looking at it as if he was unsure why he had it.

He was simply *Allen* again, and he looked down at Rez, stomping near his feet.

"That's a great costume for Vesta," he said dreamily, and he turned away as if he hadn't just sent people running for medical assistance.

There was more confusion—and screams too panicked to be part of an act—at the end of the lane, and Rez lifted his head and charged towards it.

He cursed his alarmingly tiny legs; he should be able to close the distance to the dours he could sense in moments, and instead he galloped full out at a pitiful speed for far too long as the dours did their deadly work.

CHAPTER 16

Heather lifted her skirts and pelted after the tiny unicorn Rez. He was everything he had been in her brief vision, built like a draft horse, but in perfect miniature and no larger than Vesta herself.

Before she could catch up with him, they were skidding around a corner, and Heather drew up in alarm.

Two men in costume were brawling, and they were fighting in earnest, biting each other and spitting insults as a woman spewing hate and jealous anger was systematically destroying one of the nearby booths. Customers milled about uncertainly, not sure if this was one of the acts or not.

Rez dashed in to face the combatants, but before he could react, they had tumbled onto him, pinning him helplessly to the ground. Heather gasped, watching him go under the two big men, and could only imagine how they must be crushing him.

Trying not to imagine Rez's tiny bones breaking, she dashed to haul the combatants apart and off of the little unicorn. "Stop it!" she cried. "Just stop!"

She had one of the men by the arm, and was looking full into his face when she saw it.

It was as if there was a shadow sitting over him, smothering him in darkness, with strands of smoke seeping into every pore.

And that wasn't all she saw. Beyond him, it was as if a web of strands of light was coming into focus, like trying to see them through a steam-clouded shower door. They were everywhere, thick and thin, glowing tangles, through people, into the ground, up in the air…and the shadow of the dour was avoiding them. Without thinking, Heather reached up and took one in her hand, feeling the electric tingle of it against her skin, and she brought it to touch the man she was holding, just as he raised his other fist to hit her.

He went limp in her grasp, staggering as the other fighter caught sight of Heather and moved to attack her.

Heather pulled another of the strands and tried to wrap it around the angry man.

He fell back as the darkness seemed to weaken and dissipate and Heather, weeping, moved to roll him off the struggling unicorn.

Rez looked unharmed, if more indignant than Vesta after a bath, and he staggered to his golden hooves as something shattered beside him.

Heather turned and saw a vendor she knew, Teresa, lifting one of her pottery jars into the air. She had that same crazed darkness like an overlay, and she was glaring at Heather intensely.

Heather blinked and squinted as the lines of light seemed to swim in her vision. They were all tangled together, and if she just pulled *here*...

Feeling supremely foolish, Heather reached to where one of the impossible strands ran right next to her and gave it a tug. A knot of the stuff was pulled right through Teresa, who put down the pot she was hefting as if she wasn't sure why she was holding it in the first place.

The people who had been affected milled about uncertainly, touching their wounds and their own mouths like they were drugged or in a state of half-sleep. Someone in the crowd clapped hesitantly and was joined by a half-hearted attempt from someone else. Even they knew that this was not the standard entertainment fare, and Rez himself was starting to attract attention.

"Italian Greyhound in a costume," Heather said, hastily improvising. She scooped Rez up into her arms and dropped him into her cavernous purse, dropping a curtsy as if they had just finished a performance. The scattered applause intensified briefly, and the audience dispersed.

CHAPTER 17

*R*ez found himself trapped in an assortment of strange items with a skein of yarn, half-suffocated in Heather's jostling purse, and it was a painful and humiliating reminder that he had nearly been crushed beneath the human combatants.

He had never felt such helplessness, or been so sure of his own death.

"Are you alright?" Heather asked, once they were safe in the back of her tent once again. She gently untangled Rez from the yarn and put him down on the grass-cover ground, sagging to sit beside him.

Rez shifted back into his human form. "I don't understand," he confessed. "You saved me. How?"

Sounding half-hysterical, Heather explained, "I don't know, it doesn't make sense. I saw that you were being hurt, and all I could think was that I had to help you, and suddenly, it was like there were all these glowing lines of light everywhere, all tangled together, running through people, and around them, and all through the ground.

"And I didn't really think, I just...pulled on one of them

and it made the darkness over one of those men fade away, so I tried it with the other one, and it worked. And Teresa, she was further away, but the cords were all connected, and I thought if I could yank on one, it might pull the light through her." Her voice was very small and lost. "And I guess it did?"

Rez knelt at her feet and laid his head on her knee. "Lady, you really are a powerful sorceress."

"I'm not," Heather protested with a sob. "I don't know what I did, how it worked."

"But you succeeded," Rez pointed out. "You succeeded when I could not." He was bitterly ashamed by his own uselessness, terrified by his own weakness and inability. He was smaller than a miniature *dog*, entirely ineffective.

Vesta, drawn by Heather's distress, crawled into her lap and butted her head into Heather's chest, wriggling and crooning. Rez wondered bleakly if he would be able to comfort Heather in the same manner, and he considered sourly that it might be the only kind of help he could effect in his current state.

Heather clutched Vesta close to her chest and sobbed into the tiny greyhound. Rez wanted to gather them both into his arms, but he was not certain how welcome it would be and he was not sure if he could face her rejection after his bitter humiliation.

After a moment, she gathered herself again and bravely lifted her chin. "Why are there dours *here*?"

"I don't know," Rez confessed, wishing he had any other answer for her. "Perhaps they were attracted by my release from the ornament."

"How did they get into my world?" Heather demanded. "Can we stop them?"

"I wish I knew," Rez said between gritted teeth. He was

failing, as he had failed his world, as he had fallen in this calling, and he bowed his head in defeat.

He was lost, and alone, he was in a strange world he didn't understand, and the helpless woman he'd tried to protect had rescued *him* instead.

"You saved Allen, you know," Heather pointed out, reaching out to give his face a gentle caress. "If I hadn't seen you do it, I don't think I would have known what to do."

"My power flows so strangely here," Rez lamented. It sounded like an excuse. A knight of the fallen kingdom did not make excuses.

"We'll figure it out," Heather promised. "Together. We make a good team."

Rez lifted his gaze to hers and found all the comfort that he didn't deserve. "I will protect your world," he swore. "Whatever it takes, I will save it."

"*We'll* save it," Heather corrected him.

Rez could not resist his instincts, and he leaned in close. "*We'll* save it," he agreed, and then he kissed her.

CHAPTER 18

*R*ez's kiss was as gentle as a flutter of moth wings, and it left Heather hungry for more when he paused. It was a chance for her to protest, she thought, but that was the last thing she wanted. Forgetting about Vesta in her lap, she slid her arms up around his strong neck and broad shoulders, and pressed demandingly back.

He clasped her close, and Vesta gave a yelp of protest, which sent them scrambling apart just as Beth, the owner of the booth, came through the back flap. "What on earth is going on?" she demanded. "Why don't we have a spinning demonstration going? Why are they saying that one of the blacksmiths went berserk? Did Teresa really throw a bunch of pottery? Are you all *drunk*?"

"Beth," Heather squeaked. "I'm sorry, it's been a little nuts, who knows what they put in the water? I sold two drop spindles and a punchcard of workshop classes. Is anyone badly hurt?"

Beth stared at Rez, who managed to look devastatingly handsome and completely innocent. "I...uh...don't think so. Some minor cuts and bruises, I heard. Who's this?"

Rez stood, and bowed courteously over her hand. "I am Rez, unicorn knight, defender of the fallen fae kingdom, protector of the broken crown."

Beth positively melted. "Oh, that's *good*. Tell me you're planning to put him on stage?"

"I've got a *bunch* of things to take care of today," Heather quickly said. "Would it be okay if I left a little early?"

Beth looked from one of them to the other several times, and Heather was glad that the heat in her cheeks wouldn't show. After a moment, Beth sighed. "Yeah, go on."

Heather gathered Vesta into her arms and got to her feet before Beth could change her mind. "Let's go, Rez."

They walked for the entrance, and Heather was hyper-aware of every disagreement and complaint that they overheard, occasionally even stopping to investigate. But none of the disturbances had the same tenor as their previous encounters, and then they were climbing onto a bus back to Fairburn.

The strands of light had faded away into nothing.

The apartment was sweltering again, and Heather had a moment of frustration before she remembered that she'd turned the air conditioner off, not trusting her wiring skills enough to leave it running while she was out and risk a fire. She released Vesta from her arms and went to turn it back on.

She was relieved when it grumbled back to life when she plugged it in, and she turned to find Rez standing very close behind her.

Heather had every intention of having a very serious discussion about what she'd seen and done, and what it meant that dours were here in her world, but Rez was kneeling at her feet again, in his devastating way.

"I could not protect you," he lamented.

"We're not back to that, are we?" Heather tried to keep her tone light and warm as she drew him back up.

He cupped her face in his strong hands, his touch sending little shivers of electricity down her body. "It is more than failure," he said hesitantly. "I...*care* for you. That you were in danger and I could not help you...it...scares me."

"I was pretty scared when I saw you go down under those two brutes," Heather confessed, feeling short of breath and like an overwound spring. He was standing very close, and was so very large and handsome.

But it wasn't just that he was built and beautiful...she felt like they had a connection, like she'd been called to him since before he was even a man again. She didn't believe in love at first sight, she scolded herself...but then, two days ago she hadn't believed in the fae or in unicorns, either.

"There is magic at work," Rez said.

"I haven't enspelled you," Heather protested weakly.

"I believe you," Rez said, and he bent to kiss her again at last. She slipped her arms up around his neck and melted into him, opening her mouth beneath his.

He kissed her like a force of nature, like magic itself, and Heather thought for a moment that she could see the strands of light she'd seen at the Ren Faire through her closed eyelids.

The blast of cold air against her back, his warmth against her chest, and the heat rising in her loins gave her a strange feeling of being several entirely different people at once. And all of them wanted Rez.

His arms were where she belonged, she could not be close enough, she wanted him *in* her, she wanted them *together*, the way that they *belonged* together.

"Heather of Apartment 35…" he begged. "May I? *May* I?"

Heather was already fighting the toggles on her kirtle. "You may," she said desperately. "Please do! Yes! *Now…*"

Then he leaned down, pulled all of her clothing up over her head and cast it aside, leaving her in undergarments only. Just as easily, he bent and picked her up, kissing her as he cradled her close and carried her back to the bedroom. He kicked the door closed behind him and Vesta gave a little yelp of dismay to be left out.

He laid her down on the bed, kissing and touching and caressing her until Heather was writhing and begging and tugging at him. "Rez, yes, *please…*"

Rez pulled his shirt off over his head, and Heather hungrily ran her hands over the planes of his chest and then further down into the elastic waistband of his underwear. She cupped as much of his cock as she could, and he gave a groan of need and slipped the rest of his clothing off.

For a moment, they paused, drinking each other in. He was as hot as she remembered, and his cock was thick and rigid and Heather could not keep herself from staring at it in awe.

Then Rez was on her at last, his weight making her wild with desire. Only the thin, damp fabric of her underpants separated them. She wasn't sure if it was sweat from their hot walk from the subway or the fluid of her need for him, and it didn't matter. They were both earthy and elemental in their hunger, utterly desperate for each other.

She managed to lift her hips just enough that he could wriggle the panties off of her, and then, at last—at last!— he was driving in, filling her, closer and closer and harder and faster until she was crying out in exquisite release. Rez slowed, but did not stop, drawing her up another crest of pleasure, bit by agonizing bit until he gave a great, guttural noise of surrender and she was coming again, helplessly, as he did.

They lay together a long while after, stroking each other in wonder. When Heather closed her eyes, she felt like she could see the strands of light everywhere, like tangled skeins of yarn, drifting around them.

When she eventually fell asleep in his arms, she dreamed of the bright bands, and somehow in her dream, she was knitting with them.

CHAPTER 19

They didn't nap long, but waking with Heather in his embrace was a kind of bliss that Rez had never in his wildest dreams expected to enjoy. She was soft, limp with sleep, and her curly, short-cropped hair smelled like lavender.

It was all very hard to believe, he thought, stroking the side of her face. An entirely new world, full of weird and wonderful technology. A world that hadn't been touched by darkness or dours...until he'd come. Rez frowned up at the globe on the ceiling that lit by electricity from a switch near the door.

Had the dours somehow come through *with* him? Were they attracted by Heather breaking his spell? He winced to think that he might inadvertently put her in danger, or repay her generosity by putting her at risk.

The object of his thoughts stirred and murmured, and Rez laid a kiss on her neck that made her smile and squirm.

"What time is it?" she asked, and she rolled to look at

the box with glowing numbers by the bed. "I don't usually nap, but wow, I needed that."

"If you aren't used to magic, it may be somewhat exhausting," Rez cautioned.

"To say nothing of our *other* exertion," Heather teased. They kissed, slow and full of promise, but Heather drew away with a sigh. "I want to do some Internet searches and check The Ornament Shoppe database, and if I wait too much longer, our New York dealer will be closed for the day and we'd have to wait for Monday. Let's order take-out and we'll start looking for your shieldmates."

They dressed reluctantly, pausing more than once to kiss and nearly falling back into the bed together.

Only Rez's desire to find his shieldmates kept him from dallying more.

Vesta had not taken her exclusion from the bedroom well; one of Rez's new shoes had tiny fresh chew-marks in the leather. "Oh, Vesta," Heather scolded.

Vesta did not look contrite, and she growled and stalked around with her tail down until she won treats and scratches from Rez, who could not resist her tiny wiles.

Heather opened a thin, metallic book that had only one ever-changing page, set it sideways, and began typing on the letters on one side. Rez watched, fascinated, as pictures and words scrolled past. He could read the words, but made no sense of them, and she worked so swiftly and efficiently that Rez could only shake his head in wonder.

"Glass dragon in a ring. That's getting me nowhere. The keyword *ring* is just giving me *rings*. Griffon glass ornament. Let's try spelling it gryphon-with-a-y. What did you say the other one was?"

"A firebird," Rez said, reaching out to touch the glowing screen.

"Let's try phoenix. There can't be that many phoenix Christmas ornaments."

They cycled through many different keywords, some of them over and over, on pages that Heather selected, named eBay, and Craigslist, and Facebook.

"Wait, there!"

There was a photograph of a green glass dragon framed in a glass ring, just like Rez's unicorn had been. The description of the item would have been cryptic to anyone else: "Looking for matching glass ornaments to complete a one-of-a-kind set, including gryphon, unicorn, and firebird. Makers marks: Rez, Henrik, and Tadra. Will pay any reasonable price."

"Bingo," Heather said. Perhaps it was a plea or an expression of gratitude to a deity?

"It does not list Trey or Robin," Rez said, and he didn't realize that he was squeezing Heather's shoulders until she patted his hand in reminder. "My apologies."

"There's a number," Heather said. "Let's call."

Her phone, apparently, worked *communication* magic as well, and she tapped in the code from the webpage and then paused, while Rez paced nervously.

"Is it—"

Listening intensely to her phone, Heather held up her hand to stop him.

Finally, she said brightly, "Hi, my name is Heather Jamison, I'm calling about the ornaments you were looking for. I have found...ah...the unicorn, and I'm hoping you can help my...friend Rez. Here's my number."

She rattled off numbers, then pulled the phone from her ear and punched a button.

"I had to leave a message," she said. "Hopefully this Daniella person will call us back in short order."

Rez thought he might explode in anticipation, and

Heather drew him down beside her on the couch. Vesta jealously tried to burrow between them.

"Rez," she said hesitantly. "Whatever happens, I know you want to get back to your own world and your own...er...shieldmates. I wouldn't ask you not to do that. I just...you shouldn't think that I would make you..."

"You don't want me to stay?" Rez asked, trying to make sense of what she was saying.

"I do," Heather said breathlessly. "I just don't want you to feel *obligated*. You're clearly part of something bigger, and I don't know what kind of *significance* you put on...er...what we did."

Rez thought he understood what she was saying, and wondered how much of what he was feeling was telegraphed on his face. He was deeply conflicted, because his first duty was to his world and his shieldmates...but he knew that even they could not diminish what he felt for this brave, curious woman and her strange, *good* world. He felt weirdly as if he belonged here, and as much as he longed for his shieldmates, he was not sure if he could leave Heather for them.

"Heather," he started, then he stopped, because her phone was buzzing demandingly.

CHAPTER 20

"Whoa," Heather said, looking at the screen. "Video call, okay." She thumbed a green circle and there were a few moments of black screen while Rez tried to school himself into patience.

A brunette came into view with a moment of noise like the air conditioner. "Oh, hi! I'm Daniella. Sorry to call like this. Robin thought they might be able to...um...let's start back a little further. You found a unicorn ornament?"

Behind her a voice demanded, "Is it my shieldmate or isn't it?"

Daniella shushed him.

Heather laughed weakly. "I should say that the ornament found me," she said. "Rez is here."

"Oh good," Daniella said in relief. "That definitely simplifies things. I wasn't really looking forward to explaining that you might have to kiss the ornament to break the spell and having you call the police to have me committed."

"I figured that part out," Heather said with a grin. She already liked Daniella.

"Robin wanted to do a video chat because they might be able to build a portal if they can get a good enough look at the place there."

"Robin!" Rez whispered.

He had been lurking out of the view of the phone trying to be polite even though he was clearly wild with curiosity, but Vesta had no such manners and crawled directly into Heather's lap and craned her head around to the strange voice.

"Aww!" Daniella said. "Italian Greyhound?"

Yes, Heather definitely liked Daniella. "This is Vesta. She's a rescue."

"I've got an Afghan. His name is Fabio because of his fabulous hair."

Heather giggled, but Daniella sobered. "Here, I'm going to give the phone to Robin so they can see if they can make a portal from this kind of visual."

The picture see-sawed and there was suddenly a square-faced woman with dark eyes standing on the screen. Daniella must have put the phone further away, because she could see almost all of her, from the long, dark hair to the hem of a very stiff-looking skirt near her knees. Her eyes were dark, almost black in the poor picture of the phone.

But most remarkable of all were her wings: glimmering butterfly wings sprouted behind her, fluttering slightly.

CHAPTER 21

While Heather was staring in astonishment, Rez lost his battle of willpower and squeezed in to look over her shoulder. "Robin!" he exclaimed in joy. "I have longed to see you."

"Rez!"

At the other end of the connection, there was sudden bellow of delight and a huge face crowded in behind a cross-looking Robin.

"Trey!" Rez reached out to touch the phone, minimizing the screen by accident. "I have broken it?"

Heather brought the screen back up. "No, it's fine. Don't touch."

"Trey!" Rez repeated loudly. "Are you a giant?"

"No," Robin said crossly, "It is I that have been diminished in this world." With Trey for scale, it was clear that Robin was likely as tall as Vesta: only about a foot high.

Rez reached his hand to the screen again, and stopped himself at the last moment. "I, too, have found that power flows strangely here. My magic form is also small and weak."

Rez thought that Robin and Trey both gave a significant look at Heather, but it was tricky to read that kind of thing from such a tiny scrying screen.

"It is you that released Rez from his spell, Heather?" Robin asked gravely.

"Er, yes," Heather said.

"Did you feel drawn to the ornament from the beginning?"

Heather gave an embarrassed laugh. "Yeah," she confessed. Rez smiled foolishly.

"You must be Rez's key," Robin declared.

"Oh-kay," Heather said slowly. "What does that mean?"

"This world has a significantly different flow of power than our native place, and we cannot access it without local assistance. You, and Daniella, were called to act as keys. Through you, the knights can access the magic leylines that lie dormant here."

"The glowy electric yarn," Heather surmised.

Robin frowned. "It seems that the ley lines appear differently to each different key."

"I hear music," Daniella offered from offscreen. "Like there are bunches of different voices singing different songs, and I can lead them with my voice."

"I see these tangled lines of light," Heather said. "And I can pull on them."

"With Daniella's help, I can access the power here," Trey said, smiling adoringly out of the frame.

Rez resisted the impulse to turn and smile foolishly at Heather in kind.

"There are dours here," Rez said grimly, remembering. "Several of them, working in concert, which suggests a bleak's hand. Heather was able to purge them when I proved incapable."

The parties at the other end of the line swore in concert. "We had a bleak here, but Daniella was able to slay it," Robin said soberly. "We were hoping it was alone, but perhaps it was not."

"I thought we got rid of all the dours!" Daniella said, disappointed.

"I don't understand how they have power and you do not," Trey growled.

"Could it have come from our world? Could more come?" Rez asked.

"Not at this time," Robin said thoughtfully. "The veil between our worlds only thins at the end of the year. It must have been here already, dowsing for you as I have been."

"Dowsing?" Heather murmured sideways to Rez.

"Seeking with magic," he explained. "Though it has had success enough to get this close, that suggests it has some way of tapping the magic of this world."

"Oh, like a dowsing rod," Heather said. "I've heard of that."

"There are many echoes of our own world here," Robin said, nodding solemnly. "And the bleaks would desire to cut Rez off before he can fully activate his power through his key." They gave Rez a significant look this time.

Rez understood what Robin was implying but not saying: the bleak would also be happy to kill *Heather*, in order to cripple Rez. It seemed likely that they had been seeking her, to show up at the place where she worked.

Heather asked cautiously, "Are you a fairy?"

Robin scowled fiercely. "I am a *fable*," they said through pursed lips. "Now let me see about portalling you here."

Robin bowed their head and concentrated. Heather gasped and nearly dropped the phone as a swirling crackle of light appeared in front of them briefly and then vanished.

To Rez's dismay, Robin looked winded. "I can do it," they said wearily. "But it will take a great deal of energy to make it the size of a human form. I have been spending much of my power dowsing for you and your shieldmates and I will need a few days to get back to what counts as my full strength now. Then, we can bring you both here."

"Wait, what?" Heather frowned. "Where is *here*? Am I coming back? I have two jobs and a lease. You want me to just step through a magical door and turn my back on my life for no reason?"

"It is not for no reason, lady," Trey said earnestly from the phone. "We have a duty to prepare for battle."

Robin added, "When the veil between our worlds thins, the dark forces on the other side will attempt to come through and take this world for their own."

"You've seen what dours can do," Trey said mournfully. "Now imagine them so thick that everyone wears one and lives without mercy or grace. It is an unspeakable destiny."

"What am I supposed to do with my apartment? With my dog? Where am I supposed to stay? Look, I appreciate that you've got some unfinished business or something, but I've got bills to pay."

"Let me take the phone, Robin," Daniella's practical voice said. "This is a lot to dump on her, and I should know. You guys go reminisce about battles or something, I'm going to talk to Heather for a while." The view in the screen tilted and spun, and she was once again the only person in view. "Nice to meet you, Rez."

Rez knew a dismissal when he heard one. "A pleasure," he said sincerely. He bowed his head politely and said to Heather, "I could wait in the bedchamber."

She gave him a distant nod. Rez was tempted to give her a farewell kiss, but he didn't want to presume. He went back down the hallway quietly, letting Daniella's voice fade to nothing.

He was surprised to find that Vesta came with him, prancing at his feet and jumping up on the bed with him when he lay down. He stared at the ceiling and petted her absently.

He was relieved to know that Trey and Robin were safe, for now, and most all, to have confirmation that his attraction to Heather was not a malicious spell. But her reluctance to go where they were clearly needed made Rez keenly aware that he was rudely uprooting her life…and that he did not deserve the happiness she brought him when he had so much unfinished business.

She had told him that she would understand if he returned to his shieldmates and his world…but she hadn't mentioned coming with him. Had she been trying to warn him away from becoming too attached?

It wasn't just that he craved her lush body, it was that she completed him in some fashion he'd never realized was possible. Vesta cuddled close to him, and he gathered her into his arms.

He'd fallen in love with this crazy world and this strange woman, and her tiny dog, and he didn't deserve it in the slightest.

CHAPTER 22

"Okay, I love those guys dearly, but if I have to hear another word about honor and duty and destiny, I might have to scream," Daniella said frankly. "Let me lay it out for you in twenty-first century speak."

Heather laughed despite herself. "I'd appreciate that. It's been…a little overwhelming."

"I've been dealing with these weirdos for six months and it's *still* a little overwhelming," Daniella said with sympathy. "I so hear you."

"Did you...know magic before this?" Heather had to ask. "Like, that it even existed?"

"Not even a hint," Daniella confessed. "Not in my wildest imagination. Then I saw this ornament on the shelf in a second-hand store and I had to have it. *Had* to. No choice in the matter. Like I wouldn't be whole again without it."

"Because you're Trey's *key*. Key to what?"

Daniella's expression went warm. "His key to this world. I keep trying to think of analogies, but they always fall short. He's slightly out of phase, if you want a geeky sci fi example. He can't access the magic here without local help. Has he shifted? Is his magic form pretty small?"

"Yes," Heather said, remembering the magnificent but tiny unicorn stallion that had faced down foes many times his own size. "About as big as Vesta. Why isn't he small in human form, like Robin? Does she have a key?"

"They," Daniella corrected her. "Robin doesn't have a human half, they are entirely magic, and as a construct of magic, they have no gender."

"Oh." Heather cast back, trying to remember if she had referred to Robin by pronouns. "Sorry. I saw long hair, and a skirt, and assumed…" Come to think of it, their face had been quite androgynous.

"It's a lot easier to find a skirt that fits a doll-size person than pants that aren't going to chafe or drag. And Rez has pretty long hair himself," Daniella pointed out.

Heather touched her own short hair. "Point taken," she said.

"Anyway, Rez's *human* form is undiminished, because that half of him isn't magic." She paused, then said teasingly. "Have you slept with him yet?"

Heather nearly dropped her phone. "*Excuse* me?"

Daniella laughed. "I'm sorry, I couldn't resist. I remember how it was those first couple of days, absolutely dizzy with need. It was this crazy, whole-body, whole-soul craving for him, and I thought I'd lost my *mind*. You don't have to answer about the sex, it doesn't matter. But give him a chance, because the closer you get, the better it is and the stronger you'll both be, even when you're ready to kill him for sticking a knife in the refrigerator or whatever crazy thing he thinks has insulted your honor."

She sobered. "What I really want to talk about are the things from their world. The dours, the bleaks, they're *real,* and they are evil, and I saw what they can do. I *saw* the army that was poised to come through into our world at the end of last year. I have never been so terrified in my life, and I have never known so clearly that I had to *do* something."

Daniella shook her dark hair. "They weren't prepared to meet us last time, but they will be this time, and frankly, I don't think we can stand against them alone. We won by the skin of our teeth. We haven't had any luck finding Tadra or Henrik, though we found Henrik's key. I don't want to sound needy, but I'll be honest, I nearly cried when I heard your message and it's the first ray of hope we've had in a while. We thought we'd find the rest of you sooner, and we'd just started talking about what we'd do if we *couldn't*."

Heather wanted to believe Daniella. She was earnest and genuine and so much of what she said *resonated*. It was reassuring to know that someone else had gone through the same revelations and shattering world-view shifts. But... "I'd like to help you," she said reluctantly. "I'm sort of in favor of saving the world."

She paused, but Daniella was already nodding. "I get it. There are still a lot of real-world things that need to be solved. Fae knights and protectors of broken crowns can't seem to wrap their heads around jobs and utilities and stuff."

Heather snorted gracelessly with laughter. "Yeah, that stuff."

"We've got a place you can stay here," Daniella said. "And while we'd like as much time to train with you as possible and strategize, we don't have to portal you over *this week* like Robin was threatening. When does your lease run out? Do you love your job? Can I help you get set up with something here?"

Heather's giggle was nearly hysterical. "I don't even know where *here* is. Am I committing to live in Alaska or something equally crazy?"

"Just Michigan," Daniella told her. "The weak spot in the veil to the world of darkness is in Michigan."

"Who knew," Heather said weakly.

They talked until Heather's phone battery began to wear down, about dogs and jobs. "College degree in English. I've done retail and food service, I'm good at knitting and spinning and sewing, and I'm not too proud to wear goofy costumes," was Heather's unimpressive resume.

"It's a small town with not that many great opportunities," Daniella said apologetically. "But we've got a craft store. I'll see if they've got an opening. And you won't have to worry about rent for a while, at least. Or a plane ticket, because hey, magic portals."

Heather finally hung up, shaking her head in wonder. Here she was, talking casually about uprooting her entire life, and stepping through a rift in space to help prepare for a battle with the fate of the world in the balance.

And it really wasn't the worst idea in the world. She didn't like leaving her bosses in a lurch, but what was she really giving up? Some minimum wage jobs with no real advancement possibilities? A crappy apartment with a drunk landlord?

She was being offered a chance to be a hero, to start over somewhere new, with a great—if slightly lost—gorgeous guy who absolutely adored her. How many people ever got opportunities like that? How stupid would she have to be to walk away from this chance, and how *selfish*, if she could help keep dours and worse from the world?

Vesta was nowhere to be seen, but as she walked back down the hallway towards her room, she heard Rez crooning through the half-closed door, "Who's the best little hound? Such a pretty hound, so clever."

He even liked her dog.

Heather opened the door. "How do you feel about moving to Michigan?" she asked.

CHAPTER 23

Rez had no idea what Michigan was, or where, but he knew that he was ready to go anywhere that Heather asked him to.

"What do I have to do?" he asked.

"I'm going to give notice, and we'll keep in touch with your shieldmates and Robin should be able to make us a portal when we're ready to go. I'll list my furniture on Craigslist and...start packing, I guess?"

"Heather," Rez started, and then he fell silent. He could face terrible enemies in battle without fear, but he was unskilled and inexperienced in speaking of the complications in his own heart. She was so beautiful, so trusting.

"Daniella says I'm your *key*."

They were quiet, neither speaking.

"I—"

"You—"

Rez gestured for Heather to continue first.

"I don't really know what it means," she said in a small voice. "But I'm going to give this a shot. There's...a lot at stake, and if I'm a magical combination lock to saving the world, I'm going to do my best. Tell me more about magic."

She was so brave and true that Rez couldn't speak for a moment over the pride and awe that rose in his chest. She had been patient with his unfamiliarity with her world, and now she was being fearless in the face of all the dangers of his.

"I was never the wisest of us in magic," Rez said humbly. "We could battle in our magical forms without knowing more than instinctively how to tap the leylines and use the power to make our talents work. Henrik can— could—make portals and dowse and scry with ease. I had some success with scrying, but the other skills were beyond me. Everyone who accesses the magic does so in different ways."

"Like Daniella with her voice," Heather said thoughtfully.

"Some people use chanting, or herbs and oils in particular combinations. Robin insists that it is not the ritual itself, that it's just a matter of accepting the perception of the ley lines. You can't see them, they don't exist as we do, so you have to find a way to explain them to yourself that works for you."

"I don't see them now," Heather said. "The magical yarn things."

"They are still there," Rez assured her. "What were you thinking when you did see them?"

"That I had to save you," Heather said.

Rez stopped his flinch before it reached his face. He should not need saving. He should be the one protecting his key, not the other way around. But he couldn't let Heather know how guilty he felt for his weakness and the fact that he could not help her find her access to her magic.

"I could...put myself in peril again?" he suggested lightly. "Perhaps if I attempted to battle the *subway*?"

Heather smiled. "Please don't," she said.

"Let's try something else," Rez said, drawing her down beside him on the bed.

Vesta, unfortunately, decided that this meant all of her favorite people were there to play with her.

"No Vesta," Heather scolded. "Down. Stay."

Vesta folded reluctantly backwards on tightly coiled legs, clearly ready to spring into action at their slightest inattention.

"Close your eyes," Rez commanded, and Heather shuttered her warm brown eyes obediently.

"The ley lines are all around you," he assured her. "At all times. You can always feel them, even when you think you can't; your brain just doesn't know what to do with that information."

Vesta decided that her command to stay had worn off and she chose that moment to leap into Heather's lap and lick her face.

"I can feel that!" Heather laughed, pushing the dog away gently. "Vesta, don't make me throw you out."

Vesta dashed to the other side of the bed and rolled upside down in reckless ecstasy just out of Heather's reach.

"Let's try again," Rez said, after giving the hound belly rubs. "In the bathroom."

"Oh-kay," Heather said dubiously.

"You have a mirror in there. I will attempt a simple scry and you can try to help me."

They closed a protesting Vesta outside the bathroom and Heather sat gingerly on the closed toilet and closed her eyes.

Rez concentrated, trying to grasp at the shreds of power he could sense. It was like trying to catch smoke.

Once or twice, he thought he saw flashes of light, but only the vaguest shimmer showed on the mirror, swiftly gone.

"I'm sorry," Heather said meekly, opening her eyes.

Rez slowly knelt at her feet and took her hands. "A few days ago, you knew nothing of magic. Today you single-handedly purged three dours from innocent people. You have not failed. You may be tired, we may need better direction from Robin about how to work together. Perhaps you merely need time for your mind to accept what is happening. But do not apologize. Do not for a moment underestimate your own miraculousness."

She blinked rapidly, her eyes suspiciously bright. "Daniella said it would get stronger, the closer we got." Her voice was low and careful.

Closer to this beautiful woman? He wanted her with a deep hunger that was barely sated by their previous activity. He wanted everything she offered...even if he knew he'd done nothing to earn it.

"How do we do that?" he asked gently.

"Well...I don't think you have to sleep on the air mattress tonight," Heather said shyly.

He rose to cradle her face and crush her lips against his. He could not understand why destiny would reward his failure like this, but he was utterly powerless to resist her.

CHAPTER 24

To Heather's relief, there was no sign at the Faire grounds of any dour activity all the next day, and the odd behavior of Allen had been brushed off as a bad reaction to medicine; he didn't remember any of it. Even the people who'd been injured had only the haziest of memories. Drunken brawling wasn't that unusual, and although Teresa had been witnessed breaking the pottery by dozens of people, nothing came of it, as if no one could think about the incident very clearly, so it must not be important.

It was still burned behind Heather's eyes, vivid and disturbing, and she thought that one of the creepiest parts of it was that no one seemed to notice once it was done and past.

"I'm glad the dours are gone," Heather said, as they returned to the spinner's tent.

"Robin said that they did not think many of them had had come across to this world. But their behavior indicates direction. The greater danger is that they were likely being controlled by a bleak, one that has found us and plans to stop us."

"Tell me about bleaks," Heather said. But there were customers at her tent, and she swiftly added, "Later. Duty calls."

She knew that duty was one thing that Rez would never turn down, and she smothered her doubt that *duty* was what *she* was to Rez first and foremost.

Later ended up being considerably later, when they had returned to Heather's apartment. Hot and sweaty from most of the day at the Ren Faire, they enjoyed a long, luxurious shower together that side-tracked them back to her bedroom.

Vesta, left outside the chamber, destroyed a book.

Once Rez and Heather had picked up all the chewed up pages of *The Duke's Seduction*, Heather ordered a pizza for delivery, and they sat together on the floor in the living room assuring a very dramatic Vesta that she was not going to be abandoned, and that they still loved her.

"You mentioned that you would heal Levi up if you injured him. We have stories about unicorns being able to heal things, too. Is it magic?"

"It is, but it is instinctive magic, something that comes with my form. It is not spell magic. I...probably should not have made a promise I was not sure I could keep. I cannot do it in human form."

Heather wanted to ask to see his unicorn again, for the purely selfish reason of *OMG, unicorn*! But he'd been so embarrassed by his diminished size that she didn't push the issue.

"Tell me about bleaks," she said instead.

It was almost as if the air conditioner was suddenly working at twice the efficiency.

"Bleaks are part human and part darkness, much as I am part human and part light," Rez said. "There was a man, Cerad, who was a trusted hand of the Crown. He grew jealous of the Crown's power and tried to take it for himself. When he was unable, he poisoned it instead, turning all of our world that was light to darkness. His tainted energy created dours, and the corruption of our leylines infected the people who used it, making them bleaks, creatures of power and pure evil. They have no mercy and no heart.

"We, my shieldmates and I, were made of the last untarnished light and charged to Robin to train us to protect the last of our people. By then, the Crown had fallen, and…I think we all knew that our fight was futile."

Heather was sitting facing Rez, and she rubbed his thigh with her foot. "That's not going to happen here," she insisted. "We won't let it."

"I fear…"

Ding dong.

"Pizza," Heather said, climbing to her feet. "I gotta buzz him up and scrounge up a good tip because it's three stories up and nearly ninety."

Pizza was worth the interruption. Heather had never enjoyed watching anyone eat a simple pepperoni slice the way she watched Rez.

He closed his eyes and ate it avidly, licking his fingers and oily lips in something that could only be classified as nirvana.

They demolished the pie, though Heather only ate two slices herself, and then lay in a full stupor before Daniella called to ask Heather to forward a copy of her resume and they talked for some time about rooming logistics and Vesta's needs.

They practiced magic for a while, to no particular avail. Heather couldn't see anything but the insides of her own eyelids, and Rez could cast no magic.

He didn't offer to change into a unicorn, and as much as she wanted to, Heather didn't ask him to.

CHAPTER 25

*R*ez woke a few mornings later to the sound of clicking and lay very still trying to figure it out. Heather wasn't beside him, but Vesta was sprawled in her space. It was impossible how much room she took up for a creature so minute. All four of her delicate legs were stretched out, and when she saw that Rez was awake, her tail began to whip the pillow beside her as she wriggled closer for his attention.

Rez didn't let her charms distract him from what woke him.

Click.

Click, clickclick.

Click, click…

Heather's world was filled with strange sounds and loud machines, but this was something new and different. It was organic. Not quite mechanical. It tapped out a changing pattern. And it was *inside* the apartment.

Silent from long hours of practice, he slipped from beneath the sheets and padded to the door. He had already figured out how to open it soundlessly, at just the right speed, with just a little uplift, so that the hinges didn't squeak.

The sound was coming from the living room, where the air conditioner was humming unmusically.

Click.

Click click, clickclick.

Click…click, click click…

For a while, he just watched her: the beautiful line of her neck, the soft curves of her body, her shapely legs and the curls she wore close-cropped. They had still had not had great luck in making magic together, and Rez thought that she blamed herself, but Rez knew that it was his own doubts and insecurities that held them back.

He was not sure he deserved the happiness he'd found in Heather's arms. He had *failed his world*, and he had earned no measure of the joy she brought him. "What is this that you are doing?" he asked, after watching Heather quietly for a moment.

Heather gave a little shriek and nearly dropped the strange rods she was holding wrapped in yarn. "Would you quit sneaking up on me?" she panted. "Someone your size should not be able to move around like that in an apartment this small. I'm going to put a bell around your neck if you keep doing this."

Contritely, Rez came to sit beside her. "I am sorry for startling you," he said, but he was secretly pleased by her reaction. He had worried his skills would atrophy, as soft as his life with Heather was. Vesta, who had followed him, jumped up between them on the couch.

"Haven't you seen knitting before?" Heather asked, resuming her labor. The metal rods clicked against each other swiftly. "They had knitting in the fifth century in this world. Didn't you have sweaters?"

The yarn that had appeared randomly looped on her

tools were, upon closer inspection, most of a circular cone. She was making a *hat*.

"Your talents are many," Rez said admiringly. "I knew of such an art, but never learned domestic skills."

"This explains a lot," Heather muttered, but she smiled at him. "I was packing up the closet and found a half-finished project. I figured a hat might come in handy in Michigan, and I thought I could probably finish it today."

Much of their packing had gone like this over the past several days; Heather had filled many boxes, given many boxes away, and been sidelined by half-finished projects in excess of a dozen times.

"I found a few boxes of material and patterns that I'd wanted to make into doll clothes for Julie's daughter," she told Rez. "I thought I'd finish a few for Robin, if they wanted them."

Rez watched in awe as her fingers flashed. She didn't even watch them as she worked. She was, in fact, watching Rez, who hadn't bothered to get dressed, with hunger in her eyes. He couldn't quite resist flexing a little for her, and had to laugh when she fumbled the rods and cursed, giggling. She unwound what she'd done, eyes fixedly back on her work.

Vesta, already resigned to not getting attention from Heather, clambered into Rez's lap and butted her head into his leg. He picked her up, to forestall her hard nails on his uncovered thigh, and she gave a groan of delight and flopped into him, her tail beating furiously against his chest.

"Why does this amuse you?" he asked Heather, who looked like she was about to fold over with humor, her fingers stilled in yarn.

"It's complicated," she said. "See, unicorns in this

world have a reputation for being attracted to virginal things."

Rez sniffed. "Clearly not something our worlds have in common," he scoffed.

"It's only funny because Vesta is named after the virgin Roman goddess of home and hearth. So it's...sorry, it's lame. It just amused me."

"Never apologize for laughing," Rez said sincerely. "I endeavor to always amuse you. Laughter is a salve to ears long missing the sound of it."

She gave him a look of pity and warmth. "That is the saddest thing I've ever heard," she admitted.

Rez heaved a sigh. "I have failed," he moaned theatrically. "Even in making you laugh."

Heather shook her head. "The Ren Faire really *should* have hired you. Add it to your string of titles. Rez, fae knight of the broken kingdom, *ham* of Fairburn, protector of small hounds and damsels in distress."

"Are you distressed, my lady?" Rez asked. "Because I have many methods of...comfort."

"I am *terribly* distressed." Heather abandoned her knitting altogether and crawled into his lap with Vesta, fingers running along his chest. "I'm planning a big upheaval in my life, so I might need a *lot* of comfort," she teased.

Vesta was abandoned to the floor next to the knitting as Rez gathered his key up instead. "I have a lot of...comfort to offer," he said, kissing her neck. He rose to his feet holding her, to Heather's surprise and delight. She clung to him and giggled.

He carried her back to the bedroom and shut the door on Vesta, who howled.

"This unicorn is attracted to only one damsel," he growled.

"My knight in shining armor," Heather murmured.

Rez had read enough by now to know the reference. "My lady," he said, laying her gently into the rumpled bed. "My one. My *key*."

She stilled for a moment, as if the term alarmed her, then softened again as he kissed her.

He unbuttoned her shorts, slowly kissing her belly as he shimmied them and her underwear off of her curving hips, then down past her knees and off her feet.

He kissed his way back up her legs, and she squirmed in anticipation and delight as he slowly moved towards her treasure. When he laid his mouth at her entrance and licked, carefully, she gave a muffled cry of surprise and delight.

Rez spent some time there, exploring her folds, caressing her places of pleasure and gauging what made her most frantic.

"How did you do that?" she demanded, when Rez returned triumphantly to peel off her shirt.

"I have been reading your books," Rez admitted. "You have a selection of particularly erotic novels in the table by the bed."

She giggled and pulled him close. "Did you read *The Duke's Seduction* before Vesta ate it?"

"I enjoyed that one particularly," Rez said with a grin.

"Want to act out the garden scene?" Heather invited.

When they came out, considerably later and sweatier, Vesta had taken her frustration out on the nascent hat, and there was yarn dragged around half the house.

CHAPTER 26

Julie took Heather's two week notice in stride, though she cautioned Heather sternly about throwing away her life to move across the country with a guy she'd just met.

"Not that I really blame you," Julie added, sighing over the counter at Rez.

Heather had bought him some more clothing at the second-hand store, though she wasn't sure what Michigan fashion was, besides probably colder than Georgia. It was close to Canada, so plaid seemed appropriate, and hockey jerseys. None of it could hide his amazing physique.

Julie and Heather exchanged hugs and promised to keep in touch on Facebook.

Beth was rather grumpier about the notice.

Heather felt bad for abandoning her and worried that she'd lost a friend until she showed up to collect her last belongings and turn in her badge. Beth gave her a heaping basket of yarn, a hand-carved drop spindle made of iron-wood that Heather had been coveting for months, and the number for someone who was interested in subletting the apartment for the last two months of the lease.

They also exchanged hugs, and when Heather glanced back, Beth was wiping away tears.

Rez carried out the basket for her, Vesta snuggled into his other elbow, and Heather felt excited and scared.

She was really going to *do* this, move across half the country and try to be a hero. She and Rez had continued to try using her magic, but were still thwarted. Robin seemed to think they would have more luck helping them in person and Daniella just smirked knowingly.

Rez was an old hand with public transportation by now, weaving through the crowds with casual ease and handling his own fare. He still drew considerable attention with his powerful stride and incredible good looks, but Heather had stopped being afraid that he would step off the subway landing or try to take on a car or a parking meter in noble battle.

When they arrived back at the apartment, there was a nasty note on the front door from Marcus denying her request to break the lease. He had been avoiding her since the incident with Rez, leaving passive aggressive notes instead of answering her voicemails. He still hadn't come by to collect his toolbox.

"I think he just likes to pretend he has power over me," Heather said, crumpling the note as she unlocked the door.

Rez actually growled, rolling his shoulders forward furiously. "He has no power over you," he snarled.

Heather stopped him with a hand on his arm. "I'll be gone soon enough, anyway. And maybe Beth's friend will take over the lease. He's a big burly guy that Marcus won't dare leer at. Otherwise, I'm not out *that* much and he can kiss my ass."

"I would not be happy with his lips upon your ass,"

Rez grumbled, but the corner of his mouth quirked in a smile; he was beginning to grasp modern slang, and every so often he would surprise Heather with his understanding. He was smart, not just big and gorgeous.

Vesta wriggled in Rez's arms and he set her down to prance into the apartment. It was starting to look chaotic, with packed boxes and goodwill boxes and boxes to be put in storage at Julie's house stacked in every corner. The furniture had all been photographed and posted on Craigslist, and some of the pieces were already missing.

Rez had been firm and frowned at one of the buyers who tried to lowball on the kitchen table after an agreement had already been made and Heather had ended up getting full price for it and also selling her an extra chair at a good price. Heather considered herself independent and self-sufficient, but she could get used to being with a great, ripped guy who liked to carry heavy things and scare people who were mean to her.

Robin reported that they were feeling up to strength and was impatient to get them to Michigan, but Daniella was firm that Heather should take whatever time she needed to get things settled.

"We're pretty close to being ready," Heather said, looking around nostalgically. It wasn't that she really liked the apartment, or her neighborhood, but it had been a big part of her life and she was stepping out into the unknown. "We're almost off to figure out how to save the world."

A buyer was planning to come tomorrow to take the couch, and Heather planned to wash one last load of clothes before she donated them to charity. She'd follow up with Beth's friend, maybe pass off the keys…and then she'd be off on an adventure she'd never even imagined.

Rez, sensing her mood, came to wrap his arms around

her. "You are brave and selfless," he told her. "I am in awe of your strength."

"It's my own world I'm fighting for," Heather reminded him.

"It would be easier to ignore it," Rez said sorrowfully. "I sometimes feel that is the way of most failures, simply to hope that it becomes someone else's problem, that someone else will solve it, until it is too large and impossible to discount."

It certainly would have been *easier* to pretend this was all a crazy hallucination. But Heather could not have thrown Rez out of her apartment, and kept to her ordinary life. He'd brought *magic*, with all of its possibilities, and… she shook herself before she could finish the thought.

Rez was gorgeous, and she *liked* him, maybe even more than *liked* him, but she wasn't going to call this *love* when she still wasn't sure what the rules of magic were.

"Could I...could I see your unicorn again?" she asked yearningly.

Rez looked conflicted as he put down the basket of yarn.

He'd been embarrassed by the size of his other half, but Heather had only seen the beauty and bravery of it. "You're the most amazing thing I've ever seen, in either form," she told him, turning to fill Vesta's water bowl because she didn't want to pressure him too much. She could tell he had trouble resisting her requests, and she didn't like to take advantage of that.

When she turned back, he had shifted and Heather's breath left her in an exhale of wonder.

He was no longer the size of Vesta, and Heather remembered Daniella's words: the closer they got, the more power that Rez would have. She shivered. Was she holding him back because she was afraid of how much she was starting to care for him?

He was still nowhere near the size that she'd seen in her vision, but he was waist-high now, and so graceful and perfect that Heather hardly dared to breathe.

Vesta capered forward to weave between his legs and butt her head into him demandingly. Rez lowered his head to blow at her, and she fell over on her side with her tail wagging furiously. He gently scratched her belly with his gleaming golden horn and she whined in pleasure and rolled onto her back.

Heather knelt, and Rez stepped carefully over the greyhound to walk to her.

Vesta flashed to her feet and dashed between them, scrambling into Heather's lap for attention. But Heather's focus was solely on Rez. He moved like music, his silky white mane and tail a whispering curtain as he arched his neck and danced within her reach.

She touched his horn, the side of his nose, stroked the smooth, velvety hide on his neck. "I was completely unicorn-crazy when I was a little girl," she said softly. "I used to daydream about a unicorn coming to carry me away whenever I was sad or angry. It would rescue me from my horrible life—every pre-teen girl thinks their life is horrible—and I'd finally be whole."

Rez's nose was the softest thing she'd ever felt in her life, and his breath was warm in her hand. Vesta jumped to lick him and he gave a huff like a chuckle and bumped the side of his head against the little dog fondly.

"You are so beautiful," Heather said in awe. "And you've brought *magic* to my life."

It was hard to explain how he shifted. First he glowed faintly blue, then all of his edges seemed to smudge and change, then Rez was kneeling before her, bending to kiss her as he murmured, "You *are* the magic in my life."

CHAPTER 27

Heather led Rez down into the basement of the apartment building. She was carrying a basket of laundry and he was hefting two full bags. Vesta was doing her best poor-abandoned-dog impression back in the apartment, although Rez had offered to carry her up and down the four stories of stairs.

"You spoil her!" Heather laughed. "Have you seen how fat she's getting?"

The svelte little dog was indeed starting to show a belly, but Rez could not resist it when she set her big eyes on whatever he was eating. He frequently shared scraps under the table when Heather wasn't looking.

It was terribly hot and brutally humid, and they were both sweating by the time they arrived in the cool, concrete tomb full of looming machines. Rez thought that the room encompassed the entire bottom of the apartment building, and there were pipes everywhere and storage lockers and giant tanks at the far end.

"Welcome to the laundry room," Heather said, heaving

her basket onto a tired-looking table under a flickering bank of lights.

The big square machines had heavy lids, and they lifted to reveal gaping tubs that Heather stuffed with clothing. Sweet-smelling powder was sprinkled on top, and knobs were turned and buttons pushed as Heather explained what each one did, complete with words of power: "Permanent press, tap cold, extra rinse."

She put coins into a tray and pushed them in.

There was a hiss of water, and the machine began to churn and shake. Rez was beginning to believe that this world created things specifically to mimic terrifying monsters, lacking their own. He still sometimes reached for a sword he should be used to not having.

They filled another two of the dozen or so machines. "Wait, how much powder did you put in there?" Heather asked in alarm, when Rez tried to help. "Oh, who cares. Extra rinse it is."

"Now what?" Rez asked, once three of the machines were rumbling through their duties.

"We come back later and move clean clothes to the dryers." Heather's phone gave a buzz. "Oh good, the guys from Craigslist are coming for the couch. They might need your help getting it down the stairs."

They hiked back up the stairs. Rez insisted on walking behind Heather, in part because it was a protective stance, should danger approach from behind, and in part because it gave him such a lovely view of her enchanting posterior.

She caught him grinning as they finally got to the top of the stairs. "It is so unfair how you don't get sweaty in this heat," she said, panting and pulling at the neck of her shirt.

"I would be in poor shape to sweat after just four flights of stairs," Rez scoffed, not entirely truthfully. He was not winded, but he would have to admit that he was a little damp.

"Well, I know how to make you sweaty," Heather teased him as she opened the apartment door. "If only we weren't selling the couch in a few moments."

"We could probably make one last use of the couch before it goes," Rez suggested. "I have found that your Craigslist merchants are frequently tardy."

Vesta was racing around the room in high form, ricocheting off the remaining furniture and yipping her mixed outrage at having been left behind and joy at seeing them again.

Rez was quite disappointed in the speed at which the couch buyers showed up.

"Heather?" one of them said skeptically when Rez opened the door. The other checked their phone.

"$50 takes it," Heather said from inside the apartment. She had scooped Vesta into her arms to forestall escape and the hound was wriggling furiously.

They were two athletic-looking men who attempted at first to each take an end of the couch, then sheepishly let Rez take one side while both of them together lifted the other.

They maneuvered it awkwardly out into the hall, nearly knocking down the last hanging art, and from there made it to the stairwell with a great deal of swearing and sweating on their part.

It took considerable time to navigate the three stories; the couch appeared to be heavy for the buyers, even in tandem, so they took several breaks. More than that, however, it was long and awkward to maneuver the tight turns in the stairs. Heather squeezed past them on the last stairwell to change the laundry from washer to dryer.

"Vesta needs to go out when you're done here," she

reminded Rez. She had given him the spare key to her rooms, and knew that he enjoyed accompanying the hound on her rounds.

When Rez returned from helping to heave the couch into the back of a vehicle that looked incapable of transporting it more than a block, he passed the unpleasant owner of the apartment building coming down the first stairwell.

Rez drew up in concern and looked after him. Where before the man, Marcus, had felt distasteful in nature and crudely mannered, now he seemed to trail darkness. Rez didn't trust his senses in this world, but something felt subtly *wrong*.

For a moment, he hesitated, and the man was gone around the corner, walking towards the back of the building.

Rez was divided. Follow him, attempt to find out more, or do as he'd sworn and take Vesta out?

Duty won; he had promised to walk Vesta. He was not certain in his worry, and there was no reason to think that Heather would be in danger; Marcus had not been headed down the final flight of stairs. And Rez would swear that the man wasn't dour-ridden; he knew the flavor of *that* kind of possession, even in this world.

Reluctantly, he mounted the stairs to fetch Vesta, took her downstairs and impatiently waited while she sniffed at every available place for her leavings and found them all lacking.

Rez found himself growling and pacing and when he finally scooped up Vesta's tiny offering in the plastic bag, he actually ran for the trash can with the hound under his arm. He made the three floors in record time, nearly bowling over one of Heather's elderly neighbors in his haste.

Vesta pinned her ears back in alarm, and gave her signature tremble.

The deadbolt clicked back ominously; wouldn't Heather have left it unlocked for his return if she had finished in the basement. And *shouldn't* she be done? The task had sounded simple.

Sure enough, the apartment was empty and Heather didn't answer his bellow of her name.

Without remembering to put Vesta down or lock the door again, Rez was bolting down the hallway, cursing and wishing he wasn't the only one of his shieldmates without wings.

CHAPTER 28

*H*eather heaved the last of the laundry into the dryer and fiddled with the settings. The basement was quiet without Rez's company, and it felt more than a little creepy.

It was disturbing how wrong everything felt when Rez wasn't with her.

Part of her resented it.

She was supposed to be brave and independent. She didn't need some *guy* with her to feel safe in the basement laundry where she'd been a hundred times.

And part of her loved it.

She loved how she didn't have to be constantly on the alert when he was around, confident that she was safe. Rez would do anything to protect her, and her life was better with him near.

She was more comfortable than she'd ever been in her life, tinkering around her apartment in her sleeping shirt while Rez pretended not to watch her. She loved making meals, introducing him to strange foods and new sights. It was amazing, seeing the world so fresh and unexpected through his eyes.

And most of her was terrified of her dependence and afraid of how badly she yearned for him in ways that defied logic.

But it wasn't just yearning; the basement felt outright creepy without him.

One of the fluorescents was flickering more ominously than usual, and it looked like another had burnt out entirely. Good luck getting Marcus to fix those before it was completely pitch black in the laundry room and people were threatening lawsuits, Heather thought to herself.

Then her heart lifted as she remembered that Marcus wasn't going to be her problem anymore.

It plummeted again as she remembered the scope of *why* she was moving, and all the magical baggage of suddenly being someone who could *save the world*.

That, and the fact that she had no idea how she'd done what she did, or how to do it on command.

What if she failed Rez? What if she never could learn to control the power? What if she doomed them all to—

One of the lights flickered off.

"Heather."

Heather gave a little squeak of terror and spun, backing up to the dryer in fright.

"You scared me," she told Marcus furiously, her heart racing and her throat dry.

"The key…"

"I've lined up a subletter," Heather said defensively, willing her breath back to normal. "I'll give them the key."

Was Marcus going to insist on doing a background check? Did he want to refuse the new renter? It probably wasn't worth going after her in small claims for two months of rent if she just skipped out. Wouldn't he *prefer* the income?

"You're not so special," Marcus hissed. "And you're not the only key."

"The only key?" Heather finally tamped down her flight instinct and could think again. Marcus knew she was Rez's *key*? But then...

She took a closer look at Marcus. He didn't look drunk, or even hungover, which were his two most common states. He looked almost blissful, like he'd found religion, or some really good prescription pills.

"I'm going to be a hero," Marcus said. "I'm going to be a ruler in the new world. They'll all do anything I want, because it was me, I'm the one who gave them their power here."

"Who are you going to give this power to?" Heather asked in sudden dread.

"It doesn't have a name," Marcus said dreamily. "It doesn't need a name. It doesn't want a name. It is the darkness, it is the directive. I am the power. I am the one who will win the battle."

High as a kite, Heather thought. Then she remembered Trey puzzling over the question of how the bleaks could have power when Robin didn't.

The bleak had a key.

Marcus was the bleak's key.

Did that mean Robin had a key?

Marcus shuddered and jerked forward like he was a puppet on strings.

Heather couldn't back up any further, the edge of the dryer pressing into her back. Marcus was blocking her only route to freedom. She'd always wondered if the laundry room met any kind of fire code at all. "I'm just doing my laundry," she said as calmly as she could. "Then I'll go."

"You can't go," Marcus said, suddenly sharp and focused.

He pulled a gun from his pants, something small and deadly-looking. Heather didn't know anything about guns, but her gut knew what it could do to her and terror closed her throat.

"You don't want to kill me," she stammered fearfully. *Take a breath, calm him down.* "I'll make sure you get your rent on time." She could bankrupt herself for her life, she figured...but deep inside, she was also sure that Marcus wasn't here for the money.

Marcus faltered, looking at the gun for a moment like he couldn't figure out how it was there. "Don't...want...to...kill...you..." he echoed.

"But you do..." said a new voice and all the cold and dark and creepiness of the laundry room seemed to gather into one of the steel-fenced corners by the propane tanks.

"You do want to hurt her," the darkness said. "She rejected you, she's too independent, too threatening."

Marcus slowly lifted the gun, then lowered it again. "*Hurt* her, humiliate her, not kill her."

"If you don't kill her, there is no reward," the darkness whispered.

The bleak, Heather reminded herself. This was a bleak, and as she looked fearfully past Marcus to the dark corner, she watched a dark, misty figure walk through the fence and solidify into...almost a person.

The tall bleak had swiftly shifting features, hidden in a billowing cloak. It held a sword that seemed to reflect no light.

Heather considered herself something of an expert in cloaks, and this one seemed spun of shadows, moving like not even the finest silk could in currents that didn't even exist in the airless room.

She cowered before them, trying to make sense of the odd dynamic she was seeing; why didn't the bleak kill her itself?

And why did Marcus look like he was fighting with himself as he slowly raised the gun to aim at her, setting his jaw to do the deed.

Then, at last, there was a crashing at the laundry room door and relief flooded through Heather as Marcus spun to meet this new threat.

"Meet me in battle, coward!" Rez roared, charging in. "I will show you the meaning of honor and you will learn the bitter taste of defeat!"

He was holding out Vesta, who was wriggling and wagging her tail merrily.

CHAPTER 29

$\mathcal{R}$ez could taste the evil in the air, the closer he got to the laundry room, and when he opened the door at last, the foul stench of the bleak was unmistakable.

He charged forward out of habit with the only thing he had at hand, swiftly realizing that the small dog he was holding was neither appropriate for fighting, nor safe on their battleground. He put her down on one of the still machines.

Her nails clattered on the metal boxes and Rez was chagrined that he'd been so careless as to bring her here before he focused again on the tableau before him.

Marcus may not be dour-ridden, Rez realized, he was being controlled by the bleak in some other fashion, and the man had Heather crowded back against a dryer in terror and surrender, though Rez could not identify what he held as a weapon.

The relief in Heather's eyes vanished as Marcus swiveled the harmless blunt object in his hands to point a small dark cylinder at Rez.

"Don't shoot! Don't shoot!" she cried, clearly fearing the thing Marcus was holding.

Confused, Marcus swiveled back to her and she put up her hands in defeat.

"Don't shoot!" she repeated. "You don't have to do it!"

It must be a projectile weapon of some power, Rez decided.

Laughter filled the room and threatened to suffocate them all.

"But he does," the bleak said, and it felt like the air was squeezing around them as it turned its attention to Marcus. "You will kill the key and disable the knight and there is nothing he can do."

"You are mistaken," Rez said, and he was shifting, driving forward, not at Marcus, but at the bleak.

Golden hooves rang on the hard concrete floor, and Rez saw his brave key take advantage of Marcus' momentary shock at his form to drive into him, her shoulder meeting his and knocking them both sideways.

He was not the size he should be, to gallop a few easy steps and skewer the bleak, but he was too mighty now to dismiss, and he could leap over the scuffle and charge the bleak, who dissolved at the touch of his horn.

Rez cornered hard, crashing into a barrel at the end of the room as the bleak rematerialized behind him. He reared, neighing a challenge, and focused every scrap of his rage and worry for Heather into chasing down the bleak and shredding it into pieces.

For brief moments, the bleak was tangible, and in these moments, Rez could do him damage and cause gratifying cries of pain, but striking again and again only seemed to weary himself and the bleak appeared no weaker.

Rez chased him over machines that dented and shrieked under his hooves, knocking down shelves and scattering laundry soap. One of the pipes broke when he crashed one of the washers onto its side. Water began to spray from the wall.

He speared the bleak again and again, carefully anticipating its physical moments. He kicked it hard with his puny legs.

And still the bleak did not seem to lose any power.

As fast as Rez could tear it apart, it pulled itself back together.

After a few rounds of chasing, it began to strike back, leaving red slices on his heaving white sides with its black sword.

He could spare no attention for Heather and the landlord, could only hope to keep their battle far from her, and let her use her own strength to escape.

Surely she would. She was strong and clever, and she would overcome the weak man and take her dog to safety. She would not pause for him, she would save herself.

He could not bear to think of her doing anything else.

CHAPTER 30

Marcus barely fought back, and Heather, in a blaze of adrenaline, was able to tackle him and wrestle the gun away from him. She threw it away, hearing it clatter against one of the washers and saw it bounce back on the floor, too close for comfort.

Vesta was in that direction, too, somewhere, yipping in confused excitement, but she was smart enough to stay out of the fray. Heather glanced at Rez. The unicorn, even larger than he'd been before, was charging around the room, leaping from machine to machine as he slashed at the fleeing shadow.

But the shadow wasn't only fleeing. It brought it's reflection-less sword down at Rez, and Heather was alarmed to see that while it appeared to be unharmed, Rez began to show stripes of blood, and stagger in weariness.

Why wasn't the bleak weakening? she wondered, gazing around for some kind of weapon she could join the fray with.

Her gaze fell on Marcus, who was hunched over, muttering and shaking. Had he gone mad?

Then Heather remembered what Daniella had said about how she sang to access her power. Was angry muttering his way of accessing the leylines? That seemed like Marcus. Heather closed her eyes, trying to summon the lines of light, and she felt, for a brief moment, like she could sense one.

She reached her arm out, trying to grasp it, trying to drag it through Marcus, and just when she thought she might succeed, Marcus opened his eyes and gave her a malevolent glare and laughed the bleak's laugh out of his open mouth.

Heather yanked on the elusive strand with all of her strength, pulling it straight through Marcus.

And nothing happened.

He wasn't dour-ridden, Heather thought, cursing herself. Marcus was standing now, like he'd gotten a second wind. His eyes were dark and inhuman, and he was muttering again. Rez gave a scream of pain as the bleak scored a hit on him, turned and battered the briefly tangible bleak into a dryer with his rear legs.

"You can stop this," Heather begged Marcus. "You don't have to help it. It doesn't care about you."

The bleak rematerialized, undamaged, and Heather could almost see the energy draining from Marcus.

The difference between them was suddenly stark and obvious.

Rez didn't take anything from her, he only took power *through* her. She felt better and stronger when they were together. Marcus seemed to grow weaker and paler with every strike the bleak made.

"You aren't a true key," Heather said angrily. "It promised you power, but do you really think it would *share* power with you? Look at what it's doing to you. It's just using you, and when it is done with you, you will have nothing. You will *be* nothing."

For one brief moment, she saw Marcus in his eyes, lost and afraid and weak. His mouth moved, and Heather realized that he was mouthing, "Help me."

He'd planned to kill her, Heather remembered, feeling shocky and afraid. He'd been planning to kill her because she was Rez's power in this world, even when she didn't know how to control any of it or fully help him.

And if killing her would cripple Rez, would killing him cripple the bleak?

Marcus was arguably a terrible person, but even if he'd planned to shoot her, Heather knew that wasn't a path she could ever walk. She couldn't turn her back on an innocent person, not matter what fate they'd chosen.

"Fight it," she hissed at Marcus. "Fight it with every scrap of decency you have buried in you. Fight it, dammit!"

But already, that flicker of Marcus was fading, subsumed in the darkness and despair of the bleak.

"Clever key," it said through his mouth. "This is a lock-pick, not a key. Already, he is burning out, but that doesn't matter. I have been through many of these already, they do not live long. And you, you may be clever, but you are not a good fit for your knight. You can't see what you're afraid of, and if you can't see it, you can't control it. You are a silly *child*, and your death will be my victory."

Marcus charged toward Heather woodenly, and there was the sudden clatter of tiny claws as Vesta launched herself for her mistress's assailant, barking her head off. Marcus paused to give a swift kick in her direction, but agile Vesta dodged it and danced around his feet, barking as if she was a much larger canine trying to savage him.

The bleak's shadow form and Rez had battled back

down the narrow room towards them. The fixtures over-head were losing power at an alarming rate and there was water spraying into the air from behind one of the wash-ers. A box of soap had fallen into the mess and the floor was growing foamy and slippery.

You can't see what you're afraid of, the bleak's words rang in her head.

She had seen the strands of light before she knew what they were. She'd been afraid for Rez, to the exclusion of everything else, and they seemed like the only way to help him.

Then Robin had explained what they were to her...and she'd been terrified.

She didn't want to admit how much the idea of having power frightened her, but the bleak was right about this.

All she had to do was stop being afraid.

Stop being afraid of magic.

Stop being afraid of love.

She had agreed to go to Michigan for duty, because it seemed like the right thing to do. But, though she said she accepted the role that seemed destined for her, she hadn't faced the part where she had to let go of her own fears and frailties.

She had to admit that Rez was more than just a hot guy with talented hands.

The closer you get, the stronger you are, Daniella had told her, with a knowing look.

And she'd known that Daniella didn't just mean sex. Ever since then, Heather had tried to *stop* from falling further, because she knew that there would be no return to who she'd been, before Rez, and magic and...

She looked down the laundry room as if everything was in slow motion. Rez was reconsidering his losing tactic of attacking the elusive bleak and was rushing straight at

Marcus, golden horn leveled, seeing the only victory possible, just as Heather had.

She couldn't let Rez kill Marcus, any more than she could do it herself.

That way lay exactly the darkness they were trying to prevent.

Is your world good? Rez had asked her.

It's complicated, she had answered, and that was the truth. *But it's good.* And that was the truth, too.

She couldn't help a weak man make the right choices. But she could choose.

She could choose to love Rez.

To trust her own heart, and his.

And the world around her burst into strands of light as she stepped to protect Marcus.

ez skidded to a stop as Heather fearlessly stepped into his path, then found that the floor before him had turned into a frictionless mass of bubbles and rainbow-hued puddles.

She had her hands out in front of her, her eyes closed.

For a moment, she was still, then she reached out with her fingers and began to pluck nothing from the air around her, twisting and pulling and looping as if she was knitting emptiness into shapes that only she could see.

And then, something settled over Rez's withers, stopping him cold before he could crash full-body into Heather.

For a moment, he turned his head, expecting to see some new attack from the bleak.

But the bleak was twisted in rage, collecting itself for another physical attack, and the sensation he was feeling was warm and right and full of power and magic.

Heather.

Heather was wrapping him in strands of power.

For a moment, it was like being swathed in a net of

fiber...then it settled into his skin and Rez could feel his magic-self becoming complete again at last.

It was like Heather had *plugged him in*.

From miniature to magnificent, he was suddenly everything he was meant to be, every fiber of his being crackling with power as he reared onto his hind legs and crashed down on the cement floor hard enough to crack it.

Bubbles went everywhere and the bleak charging him hesitated long enough for Rez to stretch into a full gallop in his direction.

His horn was no longer powerless, and when he speared the shadowy form, there was a scream of agony before it dissipated.

It was slower to reemerge, and Rez heard Marcus gave a cry as if every nerve ending in his body was being lit on fire.

Heather's attempt to save Marcus would be in vain, Rez feared.

Unless…

At the last moment, Rez spun on his hooves and charged at Marcus again, skipping carefully over Vesta, who was barking at everything in panic and fear.

Heather's eyes opened in surprise and dismay, but before she could stop him, Rez was standing over Marcus.

Instead of spearing him through the heart, the way he'd feared he would have to, he laid his horn on Marcus' head, and, reaching into the wellspring of power that Heather had given him, he *healed* him, the power flowing between them.

It was a terrible risk.

He was healing all the burnt out parts in Marcus' soul, and he might simply be feeding his enemy a fresh vessel to exploit against him.

But no one *whole* could house darkness like a bleak inside them.

Rez didn't stop at the superficial hurts, the damage the bleak had done, the surface pain. He went deeper, blazing into the dark places that drove the man to drink, the old hurts, the bitterness, the regrets.

He didn't wipe them away; to purge such things would be to change the man on a level that wasn't ethical or predictable.

But he could loosen their hold on him, let the strengths like mercy and kindness that he had scorned rise in him again. He could give Marcus hope again, and show him the option of grace.

He was a complicated man, and somewhere, under the anger and misery and the failed coping methods, there was *good*.

The healing power swelled around them, closing the wounds on his sides.

The bleak howled, materialized right beside Rez, and brought his black sword down at his arched white neck while he was unable to dart away.

Heather cried out in alarm and Rez could feel the strands of energy all around him shudder and flare, but it was too late—the blade was slicing down in a heavy arc...and passing right through him.

Marcus went limp and collapsed on the floor, and the bleak, with no substance, raged ineffectively, and then vanished.

The last flickering bank of lights on the ceiling gave an ominous pop, there was a flare of sparks from one of the soaked electrical outlets, and the room went still as the last running machines sank to silence, except for the sound of dripping water. Vesta stopped barking and shivered against Heather's feet.

The only source of light was Rez himself, standing over the unconscious landlord, glowing blue in the dank room.

Heather took a staggering step and sat down, and Rez felt the web of energy seep away as Vesta climbed into her lap.

For a moment, he grasped after it, afraid of being powerless again.

It answered him effortlessly, and he drew in a deep breath and let it go.

He was anchored in this world now; whatever last barrier had existed between him and Heather of Apartment 35 was gone forever.

He shivered back into his human form, and immediately regretted it as they plunged into darkness.

But it wasn't complete darkness; there was a dim red emergency light somewhere down the room, barely casting enough light to make out the dented dryers and washers and toppled tanks.

"Are you alright?" he asked, voice hoarse, as he crawled to Heather and gathered her into his arms.

She sagged into him. "Tired, now," she admitted. "I was so afraid for you."

"We have been victorious," he told her, pulling her close. "And you are amazing."

Heather cuddled close with him for a long moment and they drew comfort from each other as the water continued to gush from the pipes. Most of it swirled down the floor drains before it reached them. Vesta sighed and trembled.

She finally drew away. "Is Marcus going to be okay? What did you do to him?"

"I healed him," Rez said thoughtfully. "As far as I could. He should wake soon. I don't know how much it will fade—either the memory or the magic, but for a while, he was too whole for the bleak to have a foothold in him."

"Is that...is that what you have in me?" Heather asked in a very small voice, cuddling Vesta close. "A *foothold*?"

Rez sighed out a breath of air. "No," he assured her. "The bleak had to hold onto Marcus in order to draw energy through him. I only have to open myself. What we have, we are meant to have; it is connection, not possession. To access his power, the bleak had to force an unwilling subject."

"I don't know how unwilling Marcus really was," Heather said thoughtfully. "He was at least a little convinced that this was a great deal, that he would have power. Even if he couldn't quite literally pull the trigger."

"Bleaks are masters at manipulation. Fear and greed are their greatest tools. Never underestimate the power of those methods."

"There were no dours," Heather observed.

"It's possible we took out its only minions at the Faire," Rez suggested. "Robin thought it might be short-handed."

"This was battling a bleak without any dours," Heather pointed out. "And we almost got our asses handed to us. Are you...hurt?" she touched his sides, where the bleak had sliced his white hide. The only blood there was dry.

"Healing is a mutual power," Rez explained. "It reflects. I cannot heal without healing myself. But you are correct. The fight we look forward to will not be easy," Rez agreed grimly. The conflict had not gone as he'd expected. He moved strangely in this world, and the damage he and the bleak were able to do to each other was unexpected. He didn't understand how magic here worked, but he and Heather would learn and grow *together*.

Heather tipped her head down to butt against Vesta's. "My brave little girl," she said.

"We should leave this place. Is Marcus safe to leave here?"

"The fuse box is down here, undoubtedly someone will come investigate before too long and call an ambulance for him," Heather said, rising to her feet.

Hand-in-hand, they left the battered laundry room behind and started the long, slow climb to Apartment 35.

He had managed not only *not* to lock her door, but had left it wide open. "I'm sorry," he said, stricken. Heather had emphasized how important locking doors was here.

"You don't have to apologize for everything," Heather told him. "You just saved my life, after all."

Rez considered. "There is one more thing I must apologize for."

Heather put Vesta on the floor to scamper to her food dish as if she had not just nearly been trampled in a battle with dark forces.

"Don't tell me," she guessed, bolting the door behind them. "Are you married in your old world? I never thought to ask."

Vesta, finding her dish empty, frolicked back to them and danced around their feet.

Rez went to gather Heather into his arms. "There is no one for me but you. There never has been. But I still have to apologize. It is my fault you could not give me magic, before. I...did not trust that I deserved you and I think that is why."

Heather turned in his arms and slipped her hands up his chest and around his neck. "You thought you didn't deserve *me*? I was over here fearing that it was me being the stopper in the bottle. I was...so afraid."

"Afraid?" Rez said in surprise. "You have been nothing but fearless and bold in the face of so much danger and surprise. I brought evil to your world and you did not falter once in your willingness to face it."

"I have been terrified," Heather said. "And the more afraid I was, the more helpless I let myself feel, the more helpless I *was*. More than the dours or the bleaks, I was...afraid of you, of how I felt about you. I've never had feelings like this, so strong, so fast. It seemed impossible and unsettling, and I was afraid it wasn't real. Until..." She drew back.

"Until?" Her dear face was full of light.

"Until I thought I might lose you. To the bleak, to the darkness of the terrible circumstances we were trapped in. And then everything seemed so simple. I love you. I loved you the first moment I saw you, because how could I do anything else? This isn't duty; it's destiny. We are two parts of a bigger whole. Our purpose is bigger than either of us, and I didn't have to fear that anymore, because...because of you. Because you're amazing, and you make me amazing."

"Yes," Rez said joyously. "That's how I feel. You make me amazing. Not just the power that you enable, but you make me...whole. I feel *hope* again."

Heather's smile was sunlight and music. "My sweet fae knight," she said, leaning her forehead to his. "My fairy tale."

Rez cupped her sweet face in his hands. "You are my happy ever after," he vowed as he drew her lips to his.

Vesta, finally realizing that no one was paying the slightest attention to her, went to destroy Heather's current knitting project.

As they kissed, Rez knew that no matter how unraveled things got, he had found the woman who could put it all back together.

CHAPTER 32

"The sign says 'No Trespassing,'" Rez pointed out with concern.

"It doesn't mean us," Heather assured him as she pushed past the broken fence panel.

"It says 'Violators will be Prosecuted,'" he added, though he followed her obediently. It was more challenging for him, as the spacing had not been generous for Heather and he was considerably larger. "That sounds very bad."

"I used to play here all the time," Heather assured him. "Nobody cares, I promise. C'mon, we have to hurry if we're going to catch the last bus."

Dinner had run longer than she had expected. Between the still-fresh news of Heather's abrupt move to Michigan under a hazy pretense that Rez had gotten a job there, a very nervous Mr. Wright under the scrutiny of three daughters, Fiona's heathen doctor, and a *very* foreign unicorn knight, it had been an *interesting* meal.

By the end of it, Mama had tearfully allowed that Heather was growing up and could manage her own life, just as she could, and Mr. Wright, Fiona's doctor, and Rez had all been accepted whole-heartedly into the family.

Dessert had been buttermilk pie, and Mama hadn't permitted anyone to leave the table until it was entirely gone.

Afterwards, Heather looked at her watch. "I want to show Rez around the neighborhood a little on our way out," she said brightly, and everyone was too busy quizzing Mr. Wright about his pet chinchilla to object to their early departure.

"This used to be a pencil factory," Heather explained. "It's been abandoned since I was a kid."

Kudzu vines had grown basically up to the old building, and twined up all the walls in a dense green curtain. But inside, it was still echoingly empty. Graffiti covered every wall. Broken glass glittered in a few corners, and someone had dragged in a giant old couch that hadn't been there when Heather was younger. It looked tiny in the corner of the big space.

Rez eyed the stained, sagging couch with disgust. "Why are we here?" he asked dubiously.

"This is the only place I can think of where no one would see you," Heather explained with a grin.

"Your apartment is private," Rez said, confused.

"You don't *fit* in my apartment," Heather said pointedly.

Rez laughed as understanding washed over him. "You wish to see my unicorn again."

"Pleeeeaaaaaase," Heather begged shamelessly. "I have always wanted my very own unicorn, and now I've got one, and I never get a chance to see it."

Rez took her face in his hands and kissed her. "It does seem a shame," he agreed. He shifted so seamlessly that

Heather couldn't pinpoint the moment that his hands were no longer on her face.

A solid, soft nose was suddenly pressing one cheek, the whisper of his mane tickling her in a breeze running through the abandoned warehouse. He nickered near her ear, butted her, and then stepped back so that she could really see him.

Heather didn't know all that much about horses, but she knew a magnificent animal when she saw one, and Rez definitely qualified.

He was tall, and rippling with muscle. Pure white feathers fell over golden hooves, and his mane and tail were both long and silky. From his head jutted a golden spiral horn. His whole body seemed to glow in the dim building, and when he danced in place, Heather felt like he was filling the room with sparkling blue light.

She stroked his head and scratched at the base of his velvet ears, touching the horn with reverence. For a moment, all the tangled strands of magic seemed to brighten.

After a moment, Rez pulled away from her touch and turned his side to her.

Heather's eyes widened. "Ride you?" she guessed hopefully.

Rez snorted and nodded his head up and down.

Heather eyed his daunting side. "I'm going to need a boost," she said frankly. Before she could glance around to find something to climb up on, Rez had sunk easily to his knees.

It was still an awkward scramble to mount him, and Heather found that he was broad enough that straddling him stretched her thighs. She wound her hands into his mane and gave a gasp of alarm as he rose to his feet again.

Then he was stepping out with a gait so smooth that

Heather felt completely safe even though she was breathtakingly high in the air.

They trotted in an exhilarating figure-eight through the warehouse, and Rez bounced on all fours and whirled carefully while Heather clung to him and squeezed him with her thighs. He was perfectly responsive to her every twitch, slowing when she grew nervous, speeding up when she started to relax and enjoy the power between her legs. They flat-out galloped for a short distance, before the limitations of the warehouse made him pull up and slow to a stop.

Heather slipped her leg over, started to reconsider sliding down from this height, and somehow Rez shifted back into his human form as she was falling and caught her in his strong arms.

"That was the most amazing thing I've ever done," she said joyously.

Now that he was in human form, the warehouse was quite dark, and she was glad of his arms around her even before he added a kiss that left her knees weak.

"We should go, before we miss the bus," she said regretfully, wishing that they had time and a better place for other things. But she wasn't quite desperate enough to want to walk home, or pay for a taxi, or test the springs of the questionable couch.

The perfect gentleman, Rez gave her forehead one final kiss in promise and offered his arm. "To the bus," he said.

"I hear Michigan has some untouched forests," Heather said thoughtfully. "I would give my left foot to gallop through some of them with you."

"I will do it with joy," Rez said. "No need to pay in feet."

They crawled back out through the broken fence panel

and hurried down the suburban sidewalks for the bus stop, just arriving as it pulled into the stop.

Rez watched out the window with all the relish of his very first trip, and Heather watched him with equal delight.

She was getting ready to start the adventure of her life, with a man she would go anywhere with.

Then she grinned, because she'd found her *unicorn*, her impossible perfect mate.

And she couldn't imagine being happier.

Robin held the portal carefully, concentrating on keeping the opening wide and stable as the two knights heaved boxes and suitcases through.

"Whoops, careful!"

One of the hastily-stacked boxes toppled, spilling yarn back towards the open portal.

Heather, a curvy, dark-skinned woman, scrambled for the skeins, gathering them into her arms with her free hand. The carrier in her other hand whined in protest and began barking, catching Fabio's attention.

Not to be left out, the afghan hound bounded off his pillow and made a beeline for the action, silky tail wagging furiously. Robin, hovering just above the dog danger zone, adjusted the edges of the portal.

"Fabio, back!" Daniella called desperately. "I should have put him out, sorry!"

Heather, arms heaping with rolls of yarn and trying to keep the carrier out of Fabio's reach, only laughed. "It's okay! They'll have to meet eventually."

"This is the last of the boxes in the bedroom," Trey

said, carrying a stack of failing cardboard boxes marked 'BOOKS.'

"The bookcase still remains," Rez called a reminder from beyond the shimmering door.

"You okay, Tinker Bell?" Gwen asked quietly beside Robin.

Robin shot her a look of disgust. "I notice you only call me that when I am too otherwise occupied to kick you in the ass." The portal shivered and they turned their attention back to smoothing the edges as Ansel came through with an armful of boxes from the kitchen sprouting spatulas and serving spoons.

"You boys need help?" Gwen hollered after Trey as he went back through to get bookcases with Rez.

"We have it well in hand," Rez replied as a crash belied their confidence.

"I want my deposit back!" Heather called. "Be careful!"

"I assure you, nothing has been damaged!" Trey called.

"Much!" Rez amended.

"Well," Heather said pragmatically, "it's probably a good thing my landlord isn't as much of a jerk as he used to be."

She had reported that her landlord didn't seem to have any memory of either his possession by the bleak, or Rez's healing, but that she was cautiously optimistic that he seemed like a better person, more sober and less surly. The damage in the laundry room had been chalked up to 'vandals.'

Rez and Trey came through the portal with the heavy bookcase slung between them. Heather went back for a floor lamp, and finally said, "That's it, that's everything," as she stepped back through.

Robin gestured, felt the sluggish power of the world

respond, and the portal flickered and closed. They settled down to the coffee table as Rez and Trey hiked up the stairs with the bookcase, not as exhausted as they had feared. It had been a long, slow crawl back to power after the holiday battle, and they were grateful for every scrap of energy. Even their size seemed to be creeping back; it was challenging to keep pace with the clothing.

"We haven't really met," Gwen said to Heather. "I'm Gwen, I'm supposedly Henrik's key."

Heather and Rez both shook her hand and introduced themselves

"This is Ansel," she introduced. "He just owns this house."

"That's all," Ansel said wryly, shaking their hands as well. "I also own the second-hand shop where there is a now apparently a weak spot to another world that has lowered my property values considerably."

"We're grateful for your hospitality," Rez said sincerely, bowing over his hand.

"Let me show you to your room," Ansel offered, and they all moved to start taking boxes upstairs.

"You could have made the portal directly in their room and saved them having to haul everything up the stairs," Gwen pointed out. Her voice was light and teasing, but her sidelong glance at Robin was worried.

"And miss this chance to watch Trey take those stairs two at a time carrying heavy things?" Daniella said from her side, grinning. "Robin, don't listen to her. Come on, Heather, we'll help you carry your *lighter* boxes up."

Heather looked shyly around. "It's a beautiful house, are you sure I'm...we're...not imposing?"

Ansel was quick to say, "Quite sure. Gwen and I have been rattling around like loose marbles, and it was worse before she got here. It will be nice to have company."

"There's an empty garage that's great for sparring," Gwen said. "Since Ansel doesn't want us wrecking up The Second Hand Store practicing." She stooped to offer Robin her shoulder, but they shrugged her off and flew with their own power up the stairs as the group tramped together up to the second floor to see the rooms for Heather and Rez. Fabio was close at their heels.

"I'm just down there," Ansel pointed down the hall. "Gwen is at the other end. This used to be the master suite, so you've got your own bathroom."

"It is quite luxurious," Rez said gratefully.

"I love it," Heather said. "Thank you so much."

Fabio had followed them and all of his attention was on the cat carrier that Heather was holding. "This is Vesta," she said, putting it down on the bed and opening the door.

A tiny, delicate, gray dog sprang from the carrier and immediately there was a flurry of big dog meeting small, sniffing and whining and wagging tails. Fabio fell to his elbows in an invitation to play and Vesta launched herself from the bed to race around him.

"I think they'll get along fine," Heather said with a measure of relief.

"I'm beginning to feel left out," Gwen teased. "Here I am, no dog, no knight. You know, I really did think that I was going to find my trapped fae hero next. I've even been practicing my kiss in the mirror."

Robin landed on a dresser next to a box marked 'cosmetics and stuff,' and tried not to feel guilty. Their attempts to dowse had been less successful than using the Internet and they had found no glimmers to lead them to either Rez, Henrik, or Tadra—or the missing keys. It had been a long, frustrating half a year, and Robin had all but given up hope in finding any of the warriors they would need for the coming fight.

Trey and Rez were lifting the bookcase into place at Heather's instructions: "A little more to the left so it's centered in the space, yes, there!"

She hung Rez's unicorn ornament in the window, where it would catch the light and be out of dog's reach.

Vesta was continuing to parkour off every surface in the room to Fabio's excitement, occasionally stopping to bark at the bigger dog and roll over. She vanished under the bed and emerged from the other side to run headlong into a box of clothing.

Everyone laughed at their antics, and chattered about the weather (hotter than Heather had expected), and the house, and the nearby restaurants and stores, and Gwen and Heather shared their tales about trying to explain to their families why they had upended their lives and moved across the country.

"I couldn't exactly tell my mother it was because of a guy I haven't even met yet," Gwen said. "I mean, she has enough trouble with Internet dating, she's going to have way more trouble with 'destined for a fae gryphon-shifting knight from another world trapped in glass that by the way we haven't found yet.'"

None of them talked about the coming darkness or the weakening of the veil, or the futility of finding two fragile glass ornaments in the wide world before they could be damaged.

Trey and Rez were overjoyed to see each other again in person. Robin caught Heather and Daniella exchanging amused and delighted glances as the two knights embraced and pounded each other on the back and spoke quietly and earnestly with each other.

Ansel, clearly embarrassed by the exchange and feeling

out of place, offered loudly to make dinner and disappeared.

"I'll help him," Gwen added after a moment. She rolled off the bed gracefully and trotted out behind him.

"You are completely disgusting," Heather told Vesta, when the tiny canine jumped up to where she and Daniella were sitting. Fabio had gotten ahold of her with his tongue several times, and the smaller dog was well-coated with slobber.

"Let me show you to the practice garage," Trey offered to Rez. "Has your time in glass dulled your reflexes?"

"Let us determine that," Rez said, grinning. "Perhaps it is your time in this soft world that has weakened yours."

"It will be an unfair fight, when you so clearly started out less sharp than I," Trey jested.

"Are you all banter, or is there mettle behind your words?"

"Come test me, shieldmate."

They strode out, arms around each other fondly.

"I am so happy you're here," Daniella said sincerely to Heather. "And I know that Trey is, too."

"I'm excited to be here," Heather said, but her voice was sober. "I mean, I know that 'your world is going to be overtaken by evil' doesn't make the easiest circumstances for friendship, but...I'm glad to be here. It's nice to...not be the crazy lady in the room, you know?"

"Yeah," Daniella agreed. "It's a lot to take in, and I'm so glad to have someone who knows. I mean, Gwen and Ansel know, but they don't *know*, you know?"

"Yes," Heather said with relief. "I *know*." They smiled at each other almost as foolishly as the knights had.

Robin suspected the two women had forgotten they were there, and was trying to figure out how to get out of the room in the most discreet fashion, but Heather suddenly stood up and went to one of the boxes by the closet marked 'Sewing.'

"I brought you a few things," she said, rifling through the box, and Robin realized with surprise that she meant *them* when she turned back.

She held up a tiny knitted hat. "I have a sewing machine, so if you need anything altered...I wasn't sure how clothing worked with your wings, so I didn't make anything before I came. And I really did think it would be cold in Michigan."

Robin took the tiny hat and put it on their head. They didn't want to explain that they felt no cold, and didn't need clothing except for modesty reasons, grateful for Heather's thoughtfulness. "Thank you," they said sincerely. They turned, and let Heather get an eyeful of the wings behind them.

"They go right through?" Heather said in astonishment.

"They don't really exist," the fable explained. "I am a creature made entirely of magic, and your eyes fill in all the gaps that your brain can't explain."

"Wait," said Daniella. "You never told me that."

"You probably don't even see the same wings," Robin said knowingly.

"What do you see?" Heather asked Daniella.

"Dragonfly wings, but bigger, always slightly buzzing."

"No!" Heather said in astonishment. "I see butterfly wings, but like no butterfly I've ever seen, sort of shimmery and not really..."

"Not really there," Daniella concluded.

"It's not much different than the way you perceive magic," Robin said. "It's not music, and it's not strands of light, but that's how your mind can make sense of it."

"How do you see it?" Heather asked. "Magic, I mean. Though your wings, too, for that matter..."

Robin sat at the edge of the dresser, dangling their legs. "I don't see it at all. My brain is a lot different than yours and my senses aren't so limited. It's like trying to explain sound to someone who has been deaf since birth."

"Do you have a key? Apparently, the bleak did...sort of." Daniella was bravely petting the slobber-covered Vesta while Heather stroked Fabio's silky ears.

The canines eyed each other jealously.

"I could never do that," Robin said fiercely, stilling their legs. "Force power through someone for my own purposes? Even if they were *willing*, it would be too much for a human to bear. Marcus is lucky that you were there— that Rez was there, particularly, or his mind would have burned to nothing. It's distasteful at best and cruel at the worst. If I were to go that route, I'd be no better, and there would be no point to our fight."

The keys were quiet, grim-faced, and Heather slowly nodded. Fabio noisily licked her hand.

"But could you have a *real* key?" Heather asked. "Is it possible?"

"I don't believe that our kind has a true mirror in this world," Robin said solemnly. "You are like your knights, part magic, even if you never knew it and the magic here is different than our magic. But you don't have all-magic beings here any more. Perhaps you once did, but if they still exist, they are so well hidden we can not even call to each other any more."

They had talked about this before, with Trey, the keys, and the hapless store owner who had been swept up in the merry chaos. If they didn't have answers, they had hunches, and their hunch was that they were keyless. They were going to have to navigate this world's power themself and accept their crippled state.

The fable was a little better at it now, though every drop of energy had to be carefully accounted for. Gone were the days of parade-sized portals and casual scries. They knew their limitations now.

"Dinner!" came Gwen's cry from below.

The dogs knew the word well, and Vesta launched herself from Daniella's lap to dance around the floor with Fabio as the two keys rose to their feet.

Robin flew before them; one of the high points of this world was the quality of the food. Ansel had proved to be an excellent cook, and there was an enticing smell of dark gravy and meat rising from the kitchen.

"I've asked my boss and coworkers...er, ex-coworkers...to keep an eye out for the other glass ornaments," Heather said, as they walked down the stairs. "I don't want to claim that there's an actual ornament *underground*, but if anyone is likely to find Henrik or Tadra, it's them."

"Good," Gwen said with vigor as they walked in to where she was setting the table. "Because I am really not good at waiting, and Prince Charming is taking his sweet time in making his call."

The dogs took their places at their mistress' feet, and Ansel brought in a big plate of pot roast and a ladle of gravy. Gwen followed with a loaf of warm bread and a plate with butter.

"Oh," Heather said in delight. "I'm starting to warm up to this 'let's move to Michigan and save the world' plan. You know right how to make a girl feel at home."

"Do they also know about pizza?" Rez asked hopefully, to the laughter of the others.

Robin took a seat at the doll's table that had been set up for them on the main table and let Ansel serve them a portion of beef and a torn-off piece of homemade bread on small china plates.

Over dinner, the party talked about food, and pets, and plans for the rest of the summer. The open windows let the cooling twilight air in, and Robin felt a rush of contentment. They had two of their knights again. Two of their knights, and three keys. And Ansel, who had opened his home after his shop had been trashed.

If the open places in their hearts still cried for their missing shieldmates, there was a sense of family here that was unlike anything Robin had ever known.

It was, for the moment, a home, full of hope.

A THANK YOU

Thank you for reading my book! I hope you enjoyed following Rez and Heather through their adventures.

I am excited to announce that the ornaments I designed for this series are actually being brought to life:

…along with metal charms!

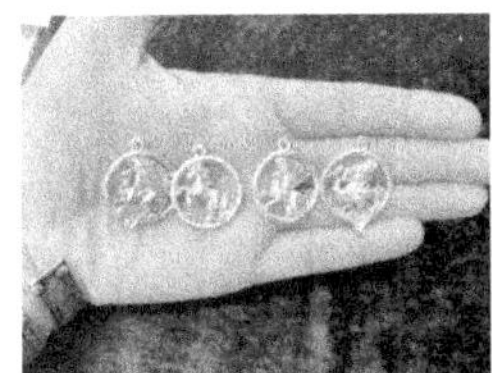

Find them at my webpage: shop.ellenmillion.com

I always love to know what you thought – you can leave a review at Amazon or Goodreads or Bookbub, or email me at elvaherself@elvabirch.com

If you'd like to be emailed when I release my next book, please visit elvabirch.com to be added to my mailing list. You are also invited to join my Reader's Retreat on Facebook, where I show off new covers first, and you can get sneak previews and ask questions.

Readers like you are why I write, and I am so grateful for all of your support.

~Elva Birch

MORE TO READ!

Want some more extra short stories? Join my mailing list for sneak previews, extras, bonus stories, and more, or join my Reader's Retreat on Facebook!

* * *

A Day Care for Shifters: A feel-good series about adorable shifter kids and their struggling single parents in a town full of mystery and surprise. Start the series with Wolf's Instinct, when Addison comes to Nickel City to take a job at a very special day care and finds a family to belong to. A gentle ice-cream-straight-from-the-container escape. Sweet and sizzling!

* * *

The Royal Dragons of Alaska: A fascinating alternate world where Alaska is ruled by secret dragon shifters. Adventure, romance, and humor! Reluctant royalty, relentless enemies…dogs, camping, and magic! Start with The Dragon Prince of Alaska.

* * *

Shifting Sands Resort (originally written as Zoe Chant): A complete ten-book series - plus two collections of shorts. This is a thrilling shifter romance set at a tropical island resort. Each book stands alone but connects into a great mystery with a thrilling conclusion. Start with Tropical Tiger Spy or dive in to the Omnibus edition, with all of the novels, short stories, and novellas in my preferred reading order! This series crosses over with *Fire and Rescue Shifters* and *Shifter Kingdom!*

* * *

Fae Shifter Knights (originally written as Zoe Chant): A complete four-book fantasy portal romp, with cute pets and swoon-worthy knights stuck in a world of wonders like refrigerators and ham sandwiches. Start with Dragon of Glass!

* * *

Green Valley Shifters (originally written as Zoe Chant): A sweet, small town series with single dads, secret shifters, sweet kids, and spinsters. Low-peril and steamy! Stand-alone books where you can revisit your favorite characters - this series is also complete with six books! Start with Dancing Bearfoot! This series crosses over with **Virtue Shifters**, which starts with Timber Wolf.

* * *

Suddenly Shifters: A hilarious series of novellas, serials, and shorts set in the small town of Anders Canyon, where something (in the water?) is making ordinary citizens turn into shifters. Start with Something in the Water!

* * *

Lawn Ornament Shifters: The series that was only supposed to be a joke, this is a collection of short, ridiculous romances featuring unusual shifters, myths, and magic. Cross-your-legs funny and full of heart! Start with The Flamingo's Fated Mate!

* * *

Birch Hearts: An enchanting collection of short stories and novellas. Unconstrained by theme or setting, each short read has romance, magic, and heart, with a satisfying conclusion. And always, the impossible and irresistible. Start with a sampler plate in Prompted 2 for fourteen pieces of sweet-to-sizzling flash fiction, or dive in with the novella, Better Half - which you can get free for joining my mailing list at elvabirch.com!

BEHIND THE SCENES

What is Patreon?

Patreon is a site where readers and fans can support creators with monthly subscriptions.

At my Patreon, I have tiers with early rough drafts of my books, flash fiction, coloring pages, signed and sketched paperbacks, exclusive swag, original artwork, photographs…and so much more! Every month is a little different, and there is a price for every budget. Patreon allows me to do projects that aren't very commercial and makes my income stream a little less unpredictable. It also gives me a place to connect with my fans!

Come find out what's going on behind the scenes and keep me creating at Patreon! patreon.com/ellenmillion

GRYPHON OF GLASS, CHAPTER 1

Ding dong!

The doorbell sent Trey and Rez scrambling for the knob, trying good-naturedly to knock each other aside with their elbows. They flung the door open so vigorously that the children outside drew back in surprise before screaming "Trick or treat!" at the top of their little lungs.

The kids were dressed in an assortment of costumes: a princess carrying a sword and wearing a wool cap in deference to the chilly air, a blue furry monster swiveling its head to see out of tiny eye holes, a mermaid with a sequined tail over her arm, two superheroes, and a knight.

"A tiny fellow knight!" Trey exclaimed in delight, and he and Rez both bowed respectfully.

The child knight looked like he was trying to decide if they were making fun of him.

"I'm Iron Man!" one of the other costumed children declared. The mermaid tried to hide behind her tail.

The two parties stood staring at each other until the blue monster asked, "Where's the candy?" in a muffled voice.

Gwen, leaning just inside the door, held the bowl out to Trey and Rez with a grin. They took fistfuls of candy and emptied them into the offered bags and plastic pumpkins.

"Truly, I thought you were jesting," Rez said, as the children tramped happily away down the walkway back to the quiet street. The unicorn shifter shook his head in wonder.

"It is a most puzzling custom," Trey agreed.

"Are you sure that adults cannot also do this?" Rez asked wistfully, watching the kids comparing treats as they returned to their trek down the street.

"It's the greatest tragedy of growing up," Gwen said mournfully. "We're going to need more candy at this rate! Where did it all *go?*"

Trey looked guilty. "The tiny sweets were very tempting."

"I picked up another bag while I was out yesterday," Ansel called from the kitchen. "Thank you, Ansel!" he joked.

"You're an angel, Ansel!" Gwen hollered back.

"No, you're the angel!"

Gwen was dressed in a flimsy white dress over leggings, a halo on her head and tiny pair of feathered wings held on with elastic.

"Beg to differ," Gwen retorted.

Ansel worked some kind of highly variably technical computer job remotely, occasionally taking long business trips to consult. The second-hand store that he owned in Wimberlette was clearly not something he required for solvency but seemed to be something he used as a way of emptying a cluttered old house that he'd inherited. Instead of complaining when a dragon broke a hole in the roof of his shop to fight horrible dark forces from another world and trashed his warehouse, he had offered a room in his home to Gwen, who had come through a portal from across the country without a wallet in her pocket and no way to get home. Heather and her unicorn-shifting fae knight, Rez, had followed from Georgia several months later. Daniella and Trey (who happened to be the dragon that had clawed through his shop roof) spent so much time at Ansel's house that he finally suggested that they simply move in and save on rent.

He only asked that they keep the space clean and the fridge stocked, and calmly converted half of his gigantic garage into a sparring space.

Rez and Trey stood watching out of the window while Gwen took the bowl in to refill. "Another troop approaches!" Trey announced with great excitement.

Ansel and Gwen exchanged an amused look and Gwen returned to the living room with the coveted candy.

The knights greeted this group with a little more decorum and happily handed out brightly-decorated candy to the squealing kids wearing an array of handmade and store-bought costumes.

The next group was already scrambling up the stairs before the last ones were gone, and for a short while, the knights were kept busy filling pillowcases and tote bags.

"It is so delightful here," Rez said, looking wistfully after the children. "So safe and happy."

"Pray we keep it thus," Trey said mournfully. The dragon shifter slung a casual arm around his shieldmate.

Gwen watched them exchange a look of sorrow and played with her sparkly tinsel halo.

Sometimes it was hard to remember the impending danger. The boundary between her world and theirs would become weaker and weaker towards the end of the year, and when it was thinnest, the darkness that had destroyed their land would try to do the same here.

Gwen had already battled the forerunners of the attack, a terrible vicious *bleak* and the evil, mindless *dours* that it led.

What's more, she had seen the army they had tried to bring through at the last New Year's Eve and it still gave her nightmares, remembering how helpless she had been against them. She, Trey, Daniella, and Robin the fable had barely been able to turn them back, and Robin had suffered greatly to seal the portals that would have let them through.

Gwen re-settled her halo, regretting the fact that she hadn't been able to do much in the scope of things. Her sword was worthless against the shadowy form, slicing through it without doing any damage. Robin swore that she would come into her power once she was united with the gryphon-shifting knight, Henrik.

The only problem was that no one knew where Henrik might be.

Four of the knights had been captured in glass and thrust into a strange world with their mentor, Robin. These ornaments, a dragon, a unicorn, a gryphon, and a firebird, had been found by Ansel...and subsequently sold, one at a time.

Gwen sometimes wondered if his generosity was a matter of apology, for not recognizing the magical glass ornaments for what they were, and for accidentally separating the four of them. But Ansel's hospitality seemed genuine, and his appreciation for their situation was not feigned; if all four knights were not freed from their glass prisons and united with their keys, there would be little to stand between the dark forces of the place they'd come from and the helpless human world.

It seemed strange that their battle had been less than a year ago, and it was terrifying to think that they were no closer now to finding the two missing knights, with New Year's looming in a few short months.

A scream shook Gwen from her musing. Trey and Rez both reached for the swords at their sides. Heather had decked them out in medieval costumes from her Renaissance Festival contacts, and they had real weapons from her blacksmith friend.

Gwen was the first one out the open door, but she knew before she got to the bottom of the porch steps that the scream was more outrage and surprise than pain.

A little brown-skinned boy was lying in the slushy snow beside the steps, holding his arm and wailing. His friends hovered over him in various states of scorn and sympathy.

"Hey there, Superman," Gwen said kindly, weaving between the kids. "Did you fall off the steps?"

"Jerry pushed me!" the little boy accused.

"I did not!" Jerry protested. "You slipped!"

"You going to want a bandaid on that?" Gwen asked, before they could argue about it further. "I bet we have some fun designs!"

The little boy brightened at the idea; he was wearing short sleeves despite the snow, and trying to crane to see his injured elbow. "Is it bleeding?"

"C'mon, I'll help you put it on," Gwen said. "The rest of you can come in and play with the dogs for a minute."

That brought them all tromping eagerly in with wet boots and laughter. Heather let Vesta down to greet them and Fabio bounded forward with his tail wagging the moment Daniella released his collar.

Vesta was a tiny Italian Greyhound, close in size to Gwen's cat Socks—who was undoubtedly hiding somewhere safe from dangerous doorbells and sticky, grabby fingers. Fabio was a full-sized Afghan Hound with a floating blond coat like the cover model he was named after. The children were immediately enthralled with both of them, and the boy holding his elbow looked like he wanted to stay and play.

"I'm Gwen," she offered, herding the hurt superhero into the kitchen. "What's your name?"

"Lawson," the little boy said sullenly. Gwen passed him a piece of candy behind her back and he brightened considerably.

"Looks like you got a little scrape," Gwen said casually as he unwrapped the treat. "Let's clean it out and I'll find a bandaid."

Lawson was inclined to snivel over the hydrogen peroxide that Gwen used, but she easily distracted him. "Did you know that I used to teach martial arts to kids just your age?" she said.

"*You* know karate?" he asked skeptically.

"I'm a black belt in Tang Soo Do," Gwen said, adding, "Fifth degree," even though it probably wouldn't mean anything to him.

He looked duly impressed. "That's cool!"

She found a tube of antibiotic and squeezed out a tiny bit to rub over the scratch, which had already stopped bleeding.

"Feeling better?" Gwen asked.

Lawson shrugged, like he'd forgotten that there had been any injury at all. "My mom has one of those!" he said, pointing suddenly at the window.

"She has the same curtains?" Gwen asked, not looking. She screwed the top back onto the antibiotic.

"The shiny glass ornaments," the small Batman explained. "But ours is yellow. And a kitty-bird."

Gwen felt her breath catch in her throat, and she nearly dropped the tube she was holding. He was pointing at the two glass ornaments hanging from the curtain rod, up out of the reach of two rambunctious dogs and an occasionally destructive cat. One was a green dragon in a ring of white, and one was a blue unicorn.

Those glass ornaments had once held Trey and Rez, imprisoned by magic.

"Like those?" Gwen said, choked. "Made of glass, with a white ring around it, and...it has wings?"

"Yeah! It's in the Christmas box. I'm not allowed to touch it. Do I get a bandaid?"

Gwen stared at Lawson for a long moment.

Henrik.

He had Henrik's ornament. Gwen felt a wave of surprise and near-panic break over her.

This was *it.* She really *was* going to get her knight…

…and everything that came with him. She was equal parts thrilled and afraid. She'd looked forward to this for so long.

"Are you okay? I want a bandaid."

Gwen shook herself. "Yeah, sure." Numbly, she fumbled the bandage box open and pulled one out. "We don't have anything cool," she apologized. "Just, er, beige."

It was pale on his mahogany-brown elbow, but Lawson looked pleased by the badge of honor anyway. "Thanks!"

When he would have sprung to his feet and rejoined his friends playing with the dogs in the front room, Gwen stopped him. "That ornament, it was part of a set, can I...uh...call your mom about it?"

"Sure!" Lawson said cheerfully and he would have left it at that if Gwen hadn't prodded him for a phone number, which he rattled off at full speed.

"Say it again," Gwen said desperately, reaching for pen and paper. "*Slower.*"

Releasing him back into the room with his friends and

the two self-declared love-starved dogs, Gwen stared at the number on the page.

Henrik.

Her...destiny?

Before she could lose her nerve, she picked up the house phone and dialed the number.

Only when the woman picked up did she realize that she hadn't asked for any names. "Is this Lawson's mom?" she asked hesitantly to the very young voice that answered.

"Hang on!"

After some garbled background conversation, someone crossly asked, "What?"

"Er, is this Lawson's mother?"

"What did he do?" she demanded.

"Nothing!" Gwen assured her quickly. "Nothing at all! Well, he fell down on our front step. I gave him a bandaid."

"He's okay?" the voice at the other end of the phone asked suspiciously.

"Fine," Gwen promised. "He screamed like a banshee, but forgot about it five minutes later."

She was rewarded with a chuckle. "Yeah, he does that. What's the problem? I need to come get him?"

Gwen paused. *I need your Christmas ornament to free a fae knight from another world* didn't seem like a successful way to start. *You have my destined fairy knight trapped in glass and I'd like him back, please* seemed, if anything, even crazier.

"I...ah...have a set of glass ornaments and it sounds like you have one of the pieces I'm missing. A golden gryphon in a white ring. A Christmas ornament. A...uh...kitty-bird." She wasn't doing a good job of not sounding weird.

Heather came swirling into the kitchen in her swishy Renaissance dress just then, oblivious to the fact that Gwen was on the phone. Vesta was tucked under her elbow and

Fabio was romping at her feet. "Hey Gwen——!" She lowered her voice considerably as she spotted the phone in Gwen's hand. "Sorry!" she whispered.

At the other end of the line, Lawson's mother said off-handedly, "Yeah, I think we got that. Amberlynn, you leave your little sister alone right this moment!"

"Can I buy it from you?" Gwen blurted. "I'll pay whatever you want. It's...it's kind of important. Part of a set, you know." Should she say it was a family heirloom? Explain more?

Heather stared at her, mouthing a question, and Gwen had to turn away and listen closely over the poor connection and the sound of her own pounding heart. Fabio, unhelpfully, came prancing to greet her and lick her hand hopefully, his nails loud on the kitchen floor.

"I'm sorry, what was that?" she asked, when she couldn't make sense of the voice.

"Yeah, sure, I could part with it. I think I paid twenty for it."

"I could come get it right now!" Gwen said desperately, before she could stop herself.

"It's in storage," the woman said.

"Tomorrow?" Gwen said, trying to keep from sounding too eager. "Let me know your address, and I can swing by whenever it's convenient."

After a pause so long that Gwen had a stab of worry that she'd hung up, Lawson's mother gave her the address of a house just a few blocks over.

"I'll bring you thirty tomorrow. *Forty!* Tomorrow afternoon," Gwen said, then she added, "I'll call first." That made her sound less creepy, right?

"Amberlynn, you let go of that child! You do not want me to——!"

This time, Gwen was sure she had hung up.

Her own hand was trembling as she returned the phone to its cradle, and she turned to find Heather gazing at her with round eyes.

"Was that…?"

"I found Henrik," Gwen said, her voice quavering like her hand had. She cleared her throat. "I found him."

"You found Henrik?" Daniella stood in the entrance of the kitchen. There was a lull in the trick-or-treaters, and her words caught the attention of the knights, who were swiftly there, demanding answers.

"Our shieldmate!"

"Where is he?"

"How did you find him?"

"What happened?"

"Is he okay?"

"How do you know?

Gwen took a deep breath to calm herself. "The kid who got hurt, Lawson, he recognized your ornaments. I got his mom's number and her address, and I'll just go and pick it up tomorrow." She managed to speak casually, like it was no big deal.

Trey and Rez gave whoops of joy, ignoring the doorbell to pound each other on the back, sweep their keys into their arms, and dance them around the kitchen. Gwen dodged back and slipped up to perch on the counter, grinning despite herself because of their contagious glee.

"Finally!" Daniella said, escaping Trey's embrace to hug Gwen. "You must be so excited."

Excitement was the smallest portion of what Gwen was feeling; she was dizzy with conflicting emotions as she hugged Daniella back.

She'd gone willingly with Robin to follow her destiny, thrilled to be part of something bigger and more wonderful than her narrow life of serving coffee and teaching little kids martial arts. The fated partner of a noble warrior, with true love like Daniella, and later Heather, had found? Yes, please!

The months since had dampened her enthusiasm as doubts crowded in: what if they never found Henrik? What if she couldn't be a proper key? What if Robin had made a mistake in finding her? The fable's power was unpredictable in this world and they admitted that they didn't have complete control over their magic.

Now she'd find out for sure if she actually measured up, and she could feel the pending judgement like a storm on the horizon.

The doorbell rang again, and the knights abruptly remembered their candy duties, excusing themselves.

"Do you have questions?" Heather asked kindly, when the three of them were alone in the kitchen.

"I don't think I have any questions," Gwen said brightly. "I kiss the ornament and bam, naked knight. Beats hiring a stripper in a cake!"

Daniella and Heather exchanged a look that Gwen couldn't quite identify. Pity, maybe? Amusement? It was definitely at her expense.

"You'll know before that," Daniella warned her. "I saw Trey's ornament and I had to have it. Like Fabio getting a whiff of steak. I was in the middle of a job orientation, and I practically shoved Ansel out of the way to get it. He must have thought I'd had a mental break or something."

"I almost accosted a customer who wanted to buy Rez's ornament!" Heather giggled. "Like, I was fully prepared to vault across the counter and start a fistfight if they didn't give it up to me."

"So don't...you know...punch Lawson's mom in the mouth when you see her, or anything," Daniella warned her with a grin.

Gwen smiled stiffly. It was a sore point with her; when people found out she had a black belt in karate, they liked to tease her about beating people up, but she'd never actually fought anyone off of a sparring mat. Twisted out of a few holds, maybe, but she stayed out of trouble for the most part and had never been in a place where she needed to prove her skills.

Not until she'd battled the bleak in Ansel's warehouse, and that had been an exercise in frustration as her physical sword had been able to do little damage to the shadowy creature.

"I'll try to avoid brawling with the woman who has already agreed to sell me the fragile glass ornament," she quipped.

Heather and Daniella both laughed with her.

"It's worth it," Heather said contentedly. "All the bleaks and dours and horrible oncoming darkness to battle, and I wouldn't trade it for the world."

There was a moment of awkward silence where they all remembered that the world might actually end with the year…and if not this year, the one after that, or the one after that.

Swiftly, Gwen said, "Well, I hope you're right, because oh my God, I will never hear the end of it from my mother if I traveled halfway across the country for a boyfriend I haven't even Internet-met and it turns out we don't actually get along."

* * *

CONTINUE the adventure in Gryphon of Glass!

www.ingramcontent.com/pod-product-compliance
Lightning Source LLC
Chambersburg PA
CBHW071322140726
47996CB00005B/1781